The Silence in the Garden

WILLIAM TREVOR

PENGUIN BOOKS

PENGUIN BOOKS

Published by the Penguin Group
27 Wrights Lane, London W8 5TZ, England
Viking Penguin Inc., 40 West 23rd Street, New York, New York 10010, USA
Penguin Books Australia Ltd, Ringwood, Victoria, Australia
Penguin Books Canada Ltd, 2801 John Street, Markham, Ontario, Canada L3R 1B4
Penguin Books (NZ) Ltd, 182–190 Wairau Road, Auckland 10, New Zealand

Penguin Books Ltd, Registered Offices: Harmondsworth, Middlesex, England

First published by The Bodley Head 1988
Published in Penguin Books 1989
1 3 5 7 9 10 8 6 4 2

Printed and bound in Great Britain by
Cox & Wyman Ltd, Reading

THE SILENCE IN THE GARDEN

William Trevor was born in Mitchelstown, Co. Cork, in 1928, and spent his childhood in provincial Ireland. He attended a number of Irish schools and later Trinity College, Dublin. He is a member of the Irish Academy of Letters.

Among his books are *The Old Boys* (1964), winner of the Hawthornden Prize, *The Boarding House* (1965), *The Love Department* (1966), *The Day We Got Drunk on Cake* (1967), *Mrs Eckdorf in O'Neill's Hotel* (1969), *Miss Gomez and the Brethren* (1971), *The Ballroom of Romance* (1972), *Elizabeth Alone* (1973), *Angels at the Ritz* (1975), winner of the Royal Society of Literature Award, *The Children of Dynmouth* (1976), winner of the Whitbread Award, *Lovers of Their Time* (1978), *The Distant Past* (1979), *Other People's Worlds* (1980), *Beyond the Pale* (1981), *Fools of Fortune* (1983), winner of the Whitbread Award, *A Writer's Ireland* (1984), and *The News From Ireland* (1986). He has also written many plays for the stage, and for radio and television. Several of his television plays have been based on his short stories. Many of his books are published in Penguin, including an omnibus, *The Stories of William Trevor*, containing five collections of stories. In 1976 Mr Trevor received the Allied Irish Banks' Prize, and in 1977 he was awarded an honorary CBE in recognition of his valuable services to literature.

The Silence in the Garden has won the *Yorkshire Post* Book of the Year Award for 1989.

for J.C.
and in memory of
my mother

CONTENTS

1. Sarah Arrives

It is 1971, and the home that has been provided for Sarah Pollexfen for so long is still a provision that is necessary. She and a one-time maid, Patty, and Tom — illegitimate son of the Rollestons' last butler — are left at Carriglas, the place that once was magical for her.

Dunadry Rectory, September 14th, 1904. 'It came from Carriglas, Sarah,' Mamma said when first I asked about the china on the sideboard. Teapot and sugar-bowl, three cups and saucers, milk jug, a single plate: pale pink roses on a white ground, the last fragments of a set that has once been grand, for ornament only now. I imagine the drawing-room at Carriglas, and the Rollestons drinking from the rosy china. I imagine the island shore where the house is, and the town you can see on the mainland. Hugh has been there. Today Hugh returned after another summer on the island and described the walk from the pier to the white gates, the scent of honeysuckle that accompanies you. He described how you round the last curve of the avenue and there the grey house is, flanked by a monkey puzzle on one lawn and strawberry trees on the other.

In old, leather-bound account books, formally lined, red lines and blue on stiff paper, Sarah has kept her diaries. Stacked beneath the window-shelf of her bedroom, they offer moments in a life. Dunadry Rectory is glimpsed, bleakly cavernous and damp, in the middle of nowhere. Her mother stitches a tablecloth in the porch, warmed by the sun through the glass. 'Never play with a bee,' she warns. 'A bee will sting you, Sarah.' Sarah's father reads to Hugh from *History of a Churchman*. 'Be so good as to attend,' he commands, 'since trouble is being taken.'

A lifetime later Sarah draws the attention of her last companions to the account books, where they are and what they contain. 'I would wish you to read them when I have gone,' she instructs. 'I promised Mrs Rolleston once.'

Carriglas, May 1st, 1908. 'Hugh's sister, are you?' the man enquired, greeting me on the platform of the railway station, and I knew at once that he was Haverty. He had the lean, narrow look of a greyhound, exactly as Hugh has described him.

How long ago it seems, even though it was only this afternoon! The train slowing, the gathering together of my belongings, the weight of the suitcases as I lifted them from the luggage rack, the narrow-faced man opening the door of the carriage. Not waiting for my answer to his question, he told me to take care. 'Yes, I'm Hugh's sister,' I said.

He called my brother Hugh because Hugh is still a child, I suppose. He observed that were it later in the summer Hugh would have been there to greet me himself, and I replied that my brother began another term at Bandon Grammar School yesterday, the Easter holidays having ended.

'You're welcome, Miss Pollexfen,' Haverty said. He carried my suitcases through the town. It was a fair step down to the quays, he said; we'd take it easy. We walked by bleak façades, through streets in which shawled women begged and children in filthy clothes ran barefoot. Men played pitch and toss, or sullenly muttered, taking no notice as we went by. When we arrived on the quays Haverty pointed across at the island — stone-walled fields above a sandy shore, bright splashes of gorse, a house looming among trees.

He rowed me across in a green boat, and when we arrived at a pier on the other side there was a horse and dog-cart

*waiting there, the horse's reins untied. At a quarter past
seven I'd had a boiled egg in the rectory kitchen and then
Father drove me in the trap the eleven miles to Bandon
railway station. Later I'd had to wait three hours in Cork
for another train, which had then been tediously slow. 'Oh,
very pleasant,' I replied when Haverty asked me what this
journey had been like.*

*The horse was allowed to pick its own way over scrubby
grass to a road whitened by dust. 'You can take the boat in
nearer to the house,' Haverty said, 'only the old landing-
stage isn't to be trusted. There's a ferryboat crosses to the
pier these days.'*

*We passed between fuchsia hedges; skylarks and swal-
lows darted high above our heads, and I wondered if there
was a cuckoo on the island. 'Cuckoo?' Haverty repeated. I
blushed, thinking suddenly that perhaps there never were
cuckoos on small islands or in this particular region of the
coast. 'Come on out of that,' Haverty called out to the
horse, which had not changed pace and did not do so now.
'We have martins that arrive up at the house,' he remarked
a moment later. 'Terrible damn pests.'*

*The high white gates which Hugh had anticipated for me
stood open at the head of a sunless avenue, with a gate-
lodge on the left. Moss and cropped grass softened the
surface beneath the horse's hooves, making our journey
eerily soundless. Beech trees curved their branches over-
head. The shiny leaves of rhododendrons were part of a
pervading greenness.*

*'Did you know the Carriglas rhododendron is famous?'
Haverty said.*

I shook my head.

'The length and breadth of Ireland, miss.'

*We came upon a house that had a gravel sweep in front of
it, running into lawns on either side. On one of these stood
the monkey puzzle, on the other three strawberry trees had
long ago been planted to form a grove, which now con-*

tained ornamental seats and a table, in white-painted ironwork. The grey façade of the house was touched with white also: the front door, the woodwork of eaves and windows. Steps and pillars introduced a dwelling that was solidly matter-of-fact, with a defiantly uncompromising note about it as though some point was being established about the durability of its stone. I remembered Mamma saying she'd always thought Carriglas would look better with Virginia creeper over it.

An elderly woman and a child came down the steps to greet me, the woman in black, her grey hair tidily drawn into a bun, the child in a red dress. Blonde plaits hung down the child's back; her eyes were so sharply blue as to seem extraordinary. Haverty shouted at the horse again, telling it to stand still, although it had already done so. Mrs Rolleston held out her hand.

'Sarah, what a wretched journey you've had! Now, please come in. This is Villana.'

Rising gently, a staircase ran around a circular hall, off which there were arched passages to left and right. A table curved with the wall that faced the hall-door, and bore a silver-framed family photograph among vases of roses. The floor was flagged; the walls were a faded green, the ornamental niches of the stairway picked out in white. Gilt-framed portraits hung above chairs with tattered covers, and on the stairway wall.

'Sherry,' Mrs Rolleston insisted. 'Before you drop down of exhaustion.'

Her hospitable manner hardly compensated for the continuing directness of her grandchild's scrutiny. The strangely intense eyes were fixed on my hat, which was grey and low in the crown. They proceeded slowly downwards to my face, lingered without interest, and then passed over my grey tweed coat. The distant cousin who had come to be a governess was poorly attired and plain, her manner affected by a diffidence that stifled charm, quite unlike her brother: unwavering in their stare, the eyes alertly reflected all they saw.

'It's awfully good of you to agree to this,' Mrs Rolleston said.

In the drawing-room there were further family portraits, and inlaid cabinets, armchairs and sofas, a gold-faced clock in the centre of a marble mantelpiece, a grand piano, and two chandeliers. Tall French windows were open to the garden, where another lawn stretched grandly, bounded by long flowerbeds. Wistaria trailed along a wall, flagstones were set around a sundial.

'My son,' Mrs Rolleston said. 'The children's father.'

My hand was shaken by a man so tall he had to stoop considerably to reach it. His face and forehead, and those parts of his head on which his fair hair had ceased to grow, were tanned and freckled. The grip that engaged my hand left it tingling afterwards.

'Welcome to Carriglas,' Colonel Rolleston said.

I wished I had been given a chance to tidy myself. I could feel grime on my palms and between my fingers. The sea wind had disturbed my hair, which I had done my best with on the train. I always have to be careful about my hair.

'Hugh,' Colonel Rolleston said. 'Is Hugh well? And your father, Sarah? Your mother?'

I said they were all well. Colonel Rolleston poured himself a drink from a decanter next to the one that contained sherry. He raised his glass, welcoming me to Carriglas again. Villana had taken a chair by one of the French windows and was swinging her legs.

'D'you remember Miss Delafinaghy?' Colonel Rolleston remarked to his mother and then he turned to me and said that Miss Delafinaghy had been a governess at Carriglas who had refused to consume fish in any shape or form, or eggs, or certain vegetables, a difficult customer all round.

'It is the privilege of governesses and nursemaids to be fussy,' Mrs Rolleston suggested. 'So you must be if you

(13)

wish, Sarah. Now, I think it would be nice if you showed Sarah to her room, Villana.'

Obediently, Villana set off, crossing the drawing-room at so rapid a pace that her father told her to slow down. We passed through the inner hall, pausing only once. 'This is my father's study,' Villana said, directing me into a tiny room with fishing-rods huddled in a corner, and fish in glass cases decorating its dark walls, and a shotgun hanging on its own. A stained velvet cloth, a shade of ochre, covered an oval table and in turn was covered with a bric-à-brac of broken ornaments and teacups, two tubes of Seccotine, cartridge cases, shoelaces, a tarnished silver plate, clothespegs and safety-pins, two paraffin lamps. 'He sits here,' Villana said, 'reading the Irish Times.'

Penetrating deeper into the house, we ascended a back stairway that had nothing of the grandeur of the front one about it, being steeply pitched and narrow, uncarpeted and with a green-painted handrail. 'The servants sleep there,' Villana announced, pointing to doors that led off a small landing, uncarpeted also. Having climbed another flight of stairs, we crossed back into the main part of the house, through an archway and down some steps. In what Villana called the nursery-schoolroom two rocking horses stood side by side in the window space, and a shelf of dolls, like a women's regiment, stretched along one wall. A speckled grey hen regarded us beadily from a cardboard box in a corner. It made a clucking sound when Villana stroked its head. She did not comment on its presence.

'And this is your own little place,' she said instead, showing me into a pink-distempered room next door. A single window looked down into a cobbled yard, across which a boy now passed with a bunch of carrots. There were stables in the yard, but no sign of horses. Chickens pecked in a corner, and in another a spaniel lay where the last patch of evening sunshine lingered.

'Thank you, Villana.' I turned away from the window as

I spoke, but Villana was no longer in the room. Through the open door I could still hear the clucking of the hen. I closed the door and sat down on the edge of the bed, allowing myself to feel weary now that I was alone. Soon after that a gong sounded.

The boy who had been in the yard was Lionel. When I arrived in the hall he was closing the entrance doors, for a moment unaware of my presence as I hesitated on the last step of the stairs. 'Ah,' he said when he turned round. Fair-haired like his father, and seeming frail, he softly introduced himself. He appeared to be as shy as I was myself.

'How are things in Dunadry?' another voice said: smiling on the stairs behind me, an older, more confident boy stood. He bowed and held his hand out. 'You're Hugh's sister,' he said. 'I'm John James.' It was he who led the way to the dining-room, saying as we went: 'Hugh's told us about Dunadry. Do you know if Bandon means the place of the pointed hills?'

I walked beside Lionel along one of the arched corridors and through the inner hall. I was confused because I did not know the answer to John James's question. He asked it again in the dining-room. 'It's Banagher, I think,' his grandmother said, 'that has to do with pointed hills.'

A butler placed a plate of curry soup in front of me, and later filled my water glass. The conversation about places and their naming continued: Carriglas meant green rock, which was what the island in certain lights resembled when seen from the mainland. A deceptive image, Colonel Rolleston pointed out, for in fact the island was fertile. Dunadry meant the place of the middle fort, Cork meant marsh. John James politely informed me that if I walked around the island I would come to a bay known as Elador's Bay, called after one of the first Rollestons. The soup-plates were removed; chops, offered with cabbage and potatoes, replaced them.

'Sarah,' Colonel Rolleston enquired, 'do you know a Mrs Trass in Bandon?'

I shook my head. My repeated ignorance embarrassed me. I felt the colour again in my face.

'Hugh didn't either,' Colonel Rolleston said. 'When I knew Mrs Trass thirty years ago she slept with corks in her pillowslip. I was only wondering if she still did.'

'Why corks?' Villana asked.

'A protection against cramp in the night. English people go in for measures like that. Mrs Trass was originally of Surrey.'

'One of the masters at school eats the shell of an egg,' John James said. 'On the grounds that it's good for his bones.'

'Does he come from Surrey?' Villana asked.

'Lincolnshire, I think. Harterblow he's called.'

'What a peculiar name!'

'English people often have peculiar names.'

There were family resemblances. The faces were spare; there was a family way of smiling. But Villana's dazzling eyes were only faintly reflected in her brothers', and the eyes of Mrs Rolleston and her son were dark and almost brooding. The children frightened me a little, even Lionel, who was so silent. 'Their mother died giving birth to Villana,' I remembered Mamma saying. 'Fortunately there was a grandmother to call upon.'

'You'll sleep well, Sarah,' Mrs Rolleston predicted after dinner. 'Everyone sleeps well at Carriglas.'

But Villana didn't want me to go to bed immediately. She led the way to the kitchen, where the butler who'd been silent in the drawing-room welcomed me gregariously. I saw him properly now: sallow-faced, black-haired, an angular, good-looking man. 'Linchy,' Villana said by way of introduction. 'Daddy stole him from a hotel in Dublin.' The butler gave his head a sideways wag and did not deny that. 'The cellars are through there,' Villana said, pointing *at a door, 'but don't ever go in. They're full of bats.' Two maids were in the kitchen, one of them sewing at the table, the other looking for something in the dresser drawers. 'A bat is harmless,' Linchy said. 'A creature of high intelligence.' At this there was a shrill protest from the maid who was sewing, an insistence that a bat would have your eyes out. An older woman – who Villana said afterwards was the cook – entered the kitchen at that moment. 'Cease that dreadful noise,' she testily ordered. The maid who was opening and closing the dresser drawers shook her head and abandoned her search. Brigid her name was, Villana said when we had left the kitchen. The cook's name was Mrs Gerrity, the maid who'd shrieked was Kathleen Quigley.*

We crossed the cobbled yard, Villana leading me to an ice-house and then through a shrubbery to the kitchen garden, where peaches ripened on brick-lined walls. We passed among apple trees to a secluded tennis-court, and continued on a path that skirted the grounds, eventually arriving at the inlet where the island's river flowed into the sea. Rhododendrons were clumped along the riverbank, a path led to the pebbled shore where a boathouse and the landing-stage referred to by Haverty were, both of them disused. In gathering twilight we reached the ruined abbey at the heart of the island, and then climbed up to the standing stones that marked a burial ground on the hill above it. Later we stood on the edge of black-rock cliffs, where there was a view of only sea and sky, darkness claiming both before we turned away. These were her favourite places, Villana said, the abbey and the standing stones and the cliffs. 'I'm looking after that hen,' she explained as we walked back to the house. 'The poor creature's far from well.'

Carriglas, May 2nd, 1908. When I came down to breakfast John James and Lionel had already begun their journey back to school in England. The places were re-arranged

(17)

around the dining-room table, Colonel Rolleston and his mother at either end, Villana and I side by side. In the nursery-schoolroom the first information I imparted to Villana was that the Romans, with their straight roads and sophisticated ways, never came to Ireland: she didn't listen. The hen gazed at us from its sick-bed and at eleven o'clock Linchy knocked on the door before entering with a tray of tea and pink wafer biscuits. Our afternoon lessons were conducted beneath the strawberry trees because Colonel Rolleston believes in fresh air.

Carriglas, June 16th, 1908. I feel less nervous now, even of Villana.

Touched in places with damp or mildew, the unadorned handwriting throws out affectionate images from the pages of the account books. The straight, tall figure of Colonel Rolleston returns from the pier with the *Irish Times*, which every morning the ferryman places in a niche of the pier wall. Sun streams through the open hall-door, rousing the Colonel's spaniel to seek the shade of the strawberry trees. Haverty stands by the dog-cart at the pier, awaiting Mrs Rolleston's return from her mainland shopping. Autumn mist lingers on the morning cobwebs in the garden. The first frost whitens the delphinium lawn.

Every year, on Villana's birthday, the children's mother is mourned, the only time Colonel Rolleston ever closes his study door. Every year there is the summer party, when croquet and tennis are played, and there is a paper-chase for the children. Four gardeners at Carriglas tend the flowerbeds and the shrubberies, and keep the avenue weeded, and the kitchen supplied. Villana's hen is buried. Letters arrive from Dunadry Rectory. There are leisurely walks to Elador's Bay and to the standing stones, and the abbey ruins. In summer Sarah's brother arrives.

The orderly household, belonging with other households of its kind, is interrupted by the regular departure of Colonel Rolleston to his regiment. He descends to the kitchen to say goodbye to Linchy and Mrs Gerrity and the maids, and then goes in search of the gardeners. His family, and Sarah too, stand on the steps to see him off. It is always a surprise when he returns, and for days afterwards in the dining-room he tells of his adventures and experiences, passing on to Linchy what news there is in Dublin, where usually he has spent a night. There is never talk of his re-marrying.

In a lesser way there is the interruption of the boys going back to school in England, and then returning. They, too, have their stories to tell; but once they are told, that is that. Even though she is so much younger, Villana is their leader again when they are back at Carriglas, organising the games they play, all of them roaming in summer over the island, climbing up and down the cliffs, discovering new caves. When, every August, Sarah's brother comes she feels more than ever a poor relation because Hugh by now belongs so easily with the family. For her own part, she is still beholden, and she has duties. She worries when the children do not return from their excursions on the island and sets out in the evening to look for them, hearing with relief their voices on the cliff path or among the rocks. In their father's absence they are reprimanded by their grandmother for the wildness of one of their games. This is an agitated entry in the diaries because Sarah has spoken to the children on the score and her strictures have been ignored. But to Mrs Rolleston she claims there'd been a misunderstanding, and in the end the matter is passed over.

'There is to be a war, you know,' Mrs Rolleston said this morning, and did not add anything to that. Linchy is courting Brigid, another diary states at a time when that war was well advanced. John James follows in his father's footsteps when he is old enough, finding himself almost at once in the trenches. There is the news of Colonel Rolleston's death. There is the news of Villana's engagement to Hugh, received after Sarah has left Carriglas and is back at Dunadry Rectory.

Carriglas does not let go of Sarah. The idyll of those years, passed with a family she came to find so attractive, haunts the grim rectory that becomes her home again. It also haunts the establishment where she is next employed. The Misses Goodbody's School for Protestant Girls is recorded as occupying a notable position in a prosperous Dublin suburb: a house built by a cooper who'd become an alderman of the city, a plain brick building, new classrooms in an annexe, a brown dining-room that smells of old bread. The Misses Goodbody are likened to elderly horses who have rummaged for their clothing at a jumble sale; Miss Fawson, who assists them, 'her lips drawn back from large teeth', is reported to utter generously whenever she has occasion to speak, as if 'keen to offer value'. Thirty-five Protestant girls at a time grow through their difficult years at the Misses Goodbody's: daughters of hardware merchants and coal merchants, of bank managers and grocers, farmers' daughters and drapers' daughters, clergymen's daughters at reduced fees. 'Tenants of a landless empire,' one of them colourfully remarks. 'We are the Jews of Ireland.' The city suburb oppresses Sarah Pollexfen, its terraces dull and similar, its hall-doors tightly closed, the blank stare of its windows seeming like eyes gone blind.

The Misses Goodbody's, March 2nd, 1919. Their two horselike heads touched over a tea-tray as they chided me. 'Ivanhoe', *the older said.* 'We would rather you read the girls *Ivanhoe* on Sundays.' *In their fusty study the dark-blue blinds are always three-quarters drawn; there is an odour of rotting flower-stems from the vases.* 'Another matter,' *the younger said.* 'The Pollack girl has been keeping a private journal. I have it here. You will take it to Mr Leary's furnace, Miss Pollexfen.' *The older smeared blackberry jam on a slice of fruitcake. Together they lifted their teacups, their grey heads close again.*

The Miss Goodbody's, June 6th, 1920. A letter from Carriglas says that Linchy has been murdered. All day long

I cannot come to terms with it. 'Bless for us this food and drink,' intoned the older Miss Goodbody this evening in the dining-room, and when her Grace ended the girls conversed in the permitted docile manner, none noticing my distress. Plates of bread were passed about, thickly cut and soaked in milk to keep it seeming fresh. Bread taken with meat must not be cut, but broken between the fingers. 'Chilly it was on the walk today,' Miss Fawson remarked, and then went on to repeat what various girls said on the walk, and how the east wind was like a wind in March, and how really one didn't know whether to wear an extra cardigan or not, and how delicious the scrambled egg was. (An opinion, incidentally, shared by no one else, certainly not by the Misses Goodbody, who were served with two platefuls of steaming haddock.) I could not concentrate on Miss Fawson's chatter, nor give my full attention to the headmistresses' ritual interrogation as to classroom progress during the day. I remembered Mrs Rolleston explaining to me what Villana had meant when she'd said that Colonel Rolleston had stolen Linchy in Dublin: he'd been a waiter in Davison's Hotel, where the Colonel often stayed. 'The children were fond of Linchy, you know,' Mrs Rolleston's letter went on. 'Your brother was too.' I remembered how the butler had told them stories about the visitors who'd stayed at Davison's Hotel, the eccentric Lord Mountbellew who liked to begin his dinner with coffee and end it with a plate of soup, and Father Ponsonby who walked in his sleep but always into chambermaids' bedrooms, and Mr Staverling of Galway who was said to be a woman. An inebriated chef's assistant had once added Vim instead of salt to a pheasant casserole. The wooden leg of a Major Flaherty had fallen from an open window and been carted away by dustmen. 'I would expect your brother to have written to you, but somehow I feel he may not have. Hugh was staying here when all this occurred; that night, all four of them had crossed over to a party near Kilmore. It was a terrible horror for them of course, but then a strange thing happened. Before he left Carriglas — it was a week after Linchy's funeral — your brother's engagement to Villana was declared to be broken off. That is the other piece of unhappy news I have to impart to you. Perhaps, on reflection, you will not find it strange.'

The Misses Goodbody's, June 9th, 1920. Hugh has not written, but today I received a letter from the rectory, imparting the information that the engagement has indeed been broken off. No reason has been given. No reason is known, as far as I can see.

When her mother died Sarah left the boarding-school and returned to Dunadry Rectory to look after her father. She cooked for him, and cleaned, and attended to the back-yard fowls — her mother's chores when she had been alive. In winter the moisture that had gathered on the inside of the rectory's window-panes froze. In autumn the gutters dripped and the dank kitchen smelt for a while of some penetrating decay. In spring the wind rattled the doors and gusted beneath the threadbare carpets on the bedroom floors. In summer Sarah walked alone on meadow paths or lanes decorated with cowparsley as lacy as the First Communion dresses of the Catholic children on their way to summer Mass in Bandon. It was then that she missed Carriglas most, as she had missed it among the suburban roads and crescents that lay about the Misses Goodbody's School for Protestant Girls. For ever, it seemed to her, she and her father would journey on Sundays in the pony and trap to Dunadry church, where his scratchy voice would deliver yet another sermon that bewildered his parishioners. For ever she would re-darn the old darns in his clothes, her only excitement the weekly shopping in Bandon.

Dunadry Rectory, November 6th, 1928. The days are heavy with the weight of their dragging. Invariably in silence, we sit over the food I cook. Father is abstracted, his thoughts occupied by the progress of his scholarship. He makes no reference to it, nor does he seek to know if I have spoken to anyone particular in Bandon. I believe I might cut my hair down to the roots and still he would not comment. It is not his way. I cannot unfairly blame him.

Dunadry Rectory, February 10th, 1929. Sometimes I hear the chatter of the girls. The brown school dining-room, with its gaslight softly hissing, seems not as awful as once I thought it. The faces of the girls pass through my mind, and one by one I attach remembered names to them. Even the towns they came from return to me: New Ross and Navan, Gorey and Sligo and Dundalk, Bruff and Thurles, Birr and Cappoquin. They came from country places too, and still I clearly see the addresses on the envelopes of their letters home, which every Saturday I inspected for smudges of ink or a poorly formed script. This evening, while serving some dish or other I had cooked, I heard again Miss Fawson's voice. It went on, and on again, about the weather. I listened with nostalgia.

'A pity there's no prettiness in her,' her father had said when she was five or six, her first awareness of a chilly truth. Yet later, when she lifted her clothes from her body and stood naked by a looking-glass, some quality was borrowed by her carelessly endowed features. In that, Sarah was certain she was not mistaken: hair and eyes, lips and nose, became part of a pleasing whole with her soft and economically distributed flesh.

This secret, shared only with herself, is a secret no longer; nor is her despair in her father's rectory. The pages of those years of resignation reveal that she believed she would not, even once again, pass through the white gates of Carriglas, nor sit beneath the strawberry trees. She believed she would not enter the drawing-room, nor see the island's fuchsia hedges in bloom, nor open the door of the ice-house, nor watch the waves breaking on the rocks at Elador's Bay. But in all those gloomy prognostications Sarah misled herself.

Dunadry Rectory, December 13th, 1930. Today my father died.

Within a month she was invited to return to Carriglas in a capacity that was not quite defined, and later was not either, housekeeper of a kind. *'Poor wretched Sarah!'* Mrs Rolleston has no doubt said. *'She'll be quite penniless.'*

That, in fact, was so; and her diaries tell how in the spring of 1931 Sarah repeated the journey she had first made almost twenty-three years earlier. She was even met, in much the same way, by Haverty at the railway station. 'I wonder what you'll think of the place these days,' he remarked, and from his tone of voice she knew at once that everything was going to be different. That, of course, was only to be expected: Villana and her brothers were no longer children; revolution had drifted into civil war since Colonel Rolleston's death at Passchendaele, though peace seemed generally to prevail now; Mrs Rolleston was approaching her ninetieth year. 'D'you remember Balt the solicitor?' Haverty said. 'He's courting Villana. Another thing is, there's talk of a bridge.'

He did not add that a child had been born to the maid who'd been searching the dresser drawers in the kitchen on Sarah's first evening at Carriglas, the child of the butler, who had not lived to marry the mother.

'You'll remember Brigid?' was all Haverty said. 'She's the cook these days, after old Gerrity was taken.' His wife was employed in the kitchen also, he said. 'A slip of a thing you'll remember her as.' He did not touch upon the woman Villana had become, nor even mention John James or Lionel, or their grandmother. She would see it all, he intimated without words: all of it was waiting for her.

2. The Bridge

———

On April 6th, 1931, work began on the construction of a bridge across the strait of water that separated the island from the mainland. That day was a Monday. In the early morning, soon after eight o'clock, the first pickaxes were driven into the ground on the mainland side, a mile to the east of the town. A breeze blew lightly, welcomed by the men as they worked. The morning would be fine, they said to one another, thankful for that also.

On the island the people of Carriglas began their day. Propped up on her pillows, Mrs Rolleston wondered if the post would bring another letter demanding money: such a communication, regularly received from Kathleen Quigley, was overdue. 'Oh God, ma'am, I've a terrible toothache,' Kathleen Quigley had once piteously complained, and she'd accompanied her to the dentist because she'd felt she should. 'Oh, ma'am, ma'am, I'll never forget how you did that for me!' the girl afterwards exclaimed. 'Not till my dying day, ma'am!' Mrs Rolleston smiled and closed her eyes again. Perhaps once, in sending the postal order, she should put a note in, a reminder of that small resolve.

In a bedroom on the same floor Villana reflected on an agreement that had been reached the afternoon before. As usual on Sunday, her fiancé had crossed on the ferry, arriving in the drawing-room at teatime. Afterwards they had walked to the standing stones. 'You are punishing yourself,' her grandmother had coolly observed a month ago, when she'd announced that she'd accepted him. But of course, no matter what it seemed like, that was quite untrue. People could conjecture as they wished, it did not signify in the least. He was nineteen years her senior; he was awkwardly stiff in his presentation and conveying of himself, like starched string, she once had thought. And for the curious she could add that she remembered from her childhood the boniness of his knees because often she had clambered on to them, attracted by his watch-chain. 'Oh, do say you'll come to Carriglas when we are married,' she had implored again on their walk the previous afternoon. 'That would mean so much to me.' And he, though remaining taken aback, had in the end agreed. That was what mattered.

In the bedroom next door John James opened an eye and at once remembered the day was a Monday, which meant he would visit the Rose of Tralee boarding-house. The thought both excited and displeased him. 'Bloody woman,' he muttered to himself, and went to sleep again.

Half a mile away Lionel began the ploughing of a field.

In the kitchen Brigid laid rashers of bacon on a pan, while in the gate-lodge at the end of the avenue the child who had been illegitimately born to her spread sugar on a slice of buttered bread. Tom had the same round face as his mother and the same dark hair. Hers was soft, like a mist about her head, his smooth and straight except for the curve of his fringe. When Tom had asked his mother about his birth – not understanding what Holy Mullihan, an older boy, had been hinting at – she'd told him that the wedding ring, and bits and pieces of furniture for the gate-lodge, had been bought; that the wedding would have taken place within a week. She'd reminded him that it was the time of the Troubles: late one night his father walked into the wires of a mine that had been trailed across the avenue of Carriglas. They'd been as good as married.

The gate-lodge kitchen, where Tom ate the bread and

drank the milk that had been left for him, was small, with a red-painted cupboard opposite the range. It contained a sink, a mangle, a table with three chairs around it, a statue of the Holy Child over one of its two doors and a picture of St Bernadette in glory over the other. A window, its frame red-painted also, looked out into an area of grass and weeds, with a privy in a corner.

Tom finished his breakfast, gathered up his schoolbooks and the two romantic novels that Miss Rolleston had given to his mother for returning to Sister Conheady's library at the convent. He bundled them into his schoolbag and left the gate-lodge, running on the road that led to the pier even though he knew he was early. He always arrived at the pier before the ferryboat had begun its journey from the quays on the other side. A couple of donkey-carts were usually there before him, their churns of milk unloaded and waiting. The donkeys would nibble the short grass, or stand patiently, until their owners returned with an empty churn from the creamery lorry. Often when they had no meal or other purchases to collect in the town, the men would wait on the island also, and the empty churn would come over on its own, in the charge of the ferryman. The island women brought their baskets of eggs to the shops on this ferry, which was the first of the day. Sometimes they brought live chickens or turkeys, which they would sell if they were offered a good enough price; if they weren't they would bring them back again. Drunk Paddy was occasionally on the early-morning ferry, but at that time of day he didn't shout at the seagulls, telling them he was penniless, like he did on the way back. Red-eyed and wild, he made the journey to the mainland when he had smoked enough fish to sell to Renehan's fish sheds on the quays. Three girls went over to work in Renehan's fish sheds and another four to attend the convent school that Tom would continue to attend himself until he was old enough to pass into the Christian Brothers'.

Neither Drunk Paddy nor any of these girls was there when Tom arrived that morning, but the usual row of churns was on the pier, the men who had brought them standing silently near by. Two women in shawls conversed quietly some distance away, their baskets at their feet. Tom climbed on to the low stone wall that protected a field where a couple of the Rollestons' cattle would graze later in the year but which now was empty. He jumped down again and kicked a pebble, trying to send it the same distance each time, moving it in a square. He heard the engines of the ferryboat cough into life, and a moment later saw it and its wake of foam.

Tom swung his schoolbag, trying not to let it touch the concrete surface of the pier. When that was no longer interesting he surveyed the familiar landscape of the town: the dark slate roofs huddled above the quaysides, the colour-washed façades like neat smudges of paint randomly arranged, the spires of two churches, one fat and seeming nourished, the other slender and more delicate. Quays and warehouses gave way to a shore, and a promenade; breakwaters staggered crookedly over sand; low, round hills began where the houses ended. Two thousand and twenty-seven people lived in the town, Sister Teresa Dolores said. There was a gasworks and a slaughterhouse, thirty-seven public houses and three banks, as well as assorted shops. There was a coal business and a meal business, and Lett's Drapery Arcade and a picture house. For years on the ferryboat Tom had heard talk of a tinned meat factory coming to the town, but it never had.

As he waited, Tom thought about the knife-throwing act that was advertised on bills stuck up on telegraph poles in South Main Street. 'Will we go?' Haverty had said to him. 'Would it be a thing yourself and myself would do?' Once, when Toft's Roundabouts and Bumper Cars had come, Haverty had taken him. They'd driven a bumper car and gone on to the roundabout, both of them sitting on a single horse. 'I never saw knife-throwing,' he'd said when Haverty asked him, and when he told his mother about it she agreed that he could go. She wouldn't like it herself, his mother said, even though it was reputed to be Ireland's greatest. *The Zodiacs* it said on the advertising bills, and this was the day they were to perform.

The ferryboat drew in and when Tom had clambered on to it he moved down to the front in order to stand beside the ferryman, which he did whenever the boat wasn't too crowded. The ferryman was old, his hairless dome as brown as the timbers of his boat, his hands massive. A navy-blue jersey stretched over a rounded chest; when it rained he wore a black waterproof and a hat that made him look like the man on the sardine tins which were sometimes stacked up in the window of Meath's grocery.

'Did you ever hear reference to an animal called The Gullet?' he enquired of a man who was crossing with a churn, and when the man replied he had not, the ferryman said he had it from Butt Nolan that The Gullet would come in at sixteen to one that same afternoon. 'If you have a coin to spare,' the ferryman advised, 'I'd place it on The Gullet with a certainty of profit.'

Nothing more was said on the journey to the mainland. Because of the noise of the engines, the fish-shed girls and the convent girls did not speak, nor did the women with their baskets, nor did the ferryman, nor the men with the churns. When the boat had edged its way in to the quay, after its engines had dwindled and the ropes were thrown and tied, the ferryman lit a cigarette and the island women exchanged remarks about the fineness of the morning with the men on the creamery lorry. Loitering, Tom watched the exchange of the full churns for the empty ones, and the arrival of a bale of barbed wire and two calves for transportation to the island. He didn't want to walk through the town with the four convent girls, which was sometimes unavoidable if they fell into step with him. When they were well ahead he began on the journey himself, turning off the quays into Narrow Lane. They were senior girls at the convent, years older than himself.

'That's a nice morning,' remarked the shopman from the London and Newcastle Tea Company in South Main Street. Tom replied, saying he hoped the bright weather would keep up. 'Ah, it will of course,' the man predicted.

Sergeant Kealy propped his bicycle against the lamp-post outside the Guards' barracks and bent down to take off his bicycle clips. Horses and carts rattled back from the creamery with empty churns, returning to the farms they'd come from. The green wooden shutters had not yet been lifted down from the windows of Meath's nor the red ones from Dungan's. The windows of the public houses were empty except for notices that said *Guinness is Good for You* and *John Jameson*. Padlocks secured the doors of Traynor's Picture Palace.

Further along the street, past Spillane's public house and Barry's confectionery and tobacconist's, Mr Coyne was unlocking the petrol pump outside Jas. Coyne Motors. He didn't notice Tom, but a shawled woman carrying baskets of fish asked him how his mother was. 'Ah, the poor creature,' she said when he replied that his mother was all right. She always asked the same question and made the same comment, and Tom often wondered why she did so. 'Hey, mister,' Humpy Geehan called across the street at him, which was what Humpy Geehan shouted at everyone, being half-witted as well as deformed. Briscoe, the porter at the Provincial Bank, sauntered to work, a cigarette hanging from his mouth.

In the yard at the convent Tom looked around for someone to play with, but only the girls from the island were there, whispering in a corner. If Sister Sullivan saw him she'd say he should sit in the classroom and go over his spellings or his tables even though, when all the others arrived, they'd be allowed to play about outside until the bell went. 'Didn't I tell you to go to the classroom?' Sister Sullivan had reminded him crossly once, after he'd run out to join them, and Tom had felt that that was unfair. He sat on the ledge outside the cloakroom, with his schoolbag beside him, his presence hidden from the windows of the classrooms. He wondered why Sister Sullivan looked at him in that dead way sometimes, as if he had done something wrong. Sister Sullivan was the oldest of the teaching nuns and considered to be the crossest.

'I like the dog,' Sister Teresa Dolores said later, standing by the blackboard. 'Now, give me that perfectly, please.'

The class tried to translate the sentence into Irish, but were not successful. Sister Teresa Dolores deplored her pupils' efforts and wrote the correct version on the blackboard. They repeated it all together, and then repeated it again. Sister Teresa Dolores hung her chart up on the blackboard, with a picture of a rabbit on it, and a picture of a black cat and a blue door and a window. Her pupils learnt the Irish for these nouns and adjectives, writing the words down in their jotters. When the bell went they forgot them.

Father Pierce came that morning, a special visit, to examine them in catechism. 'That's a great dress you're wearing,' he said to one girl, and enquired about a boy's glasses, asking him if he could see better these days and then trying them on himself to make the class laugh. Father Pierce had something to say to everyone. 'Your father made a great job of the table in the rectory,' he remarked to a boy whose father was a French polisher. 'There isn't a man in County Cork can get a gloss on to a table like your father.' He inclined his head, slowly wagging it in a complimentary way. He was a big, laughy man, his smooth black hair brushed straight back from his forehead, shiny with the oil he put on it. 'There isn't a man in County Cork,' he told a girl, 'can cut out a clerical suit like your uncle in Castlemartyr.' He made Joey Feerick sing a verse of a song. Joey Feerick was another John McCormack, he said.

The Protestant boy, Derek Birthistle, didn't remain in the classroom for the catechism examinations, and he didn't come into prayers either. He waited in the cloakroom, and once when a girl complained that a pair of scissors was missing from her schoolbag Derek Birthistle was sent for by Sister Sullivan because the schoolbag had been hanging in the cloakroom and he'd been sitting beside it for three-quarters of an hour. But Derek Birthistle hadn't taken the scissors: it turned out in the end that there hadn't been a pair of scissors in the girl's schoolbag at all. The girl had developed the habit of telling lies, and her parents said the nuns should have known they wouldn't have the money for buying scissors.

'Tell Derek Birthistle to come in now,' Father Pierce commanded at the end of the catechism examination, when Joey Feerick had finished singing. While everyone was waiting he asked a few more catechism questions. Then he said:

'Well, Derek, I hear your father did great work over in Dungarvan last week.'

Mr Birthistle was a clerk in Burke's the auctioneers and was often to be seen carrying papers on the quays, hurrying between Burke's warehouse and the office where he worked. He was small, with a waistcoat, and he had the same clever eyes as his son. Derek Birthistle was the cleverest boy in the class, but it wasn't because of that that the nuns and Father Pierce reserved a special manner for him. They wanted to save him from perdition, Tom heard a girl saying one day: you moved an inch nearer heaven if you saved a soul from hell.

'Well, we had a great time with the catechism, Derek,' Father Pierce said now. 'Were you all right in the cloakroom?'

'I was, Father.'

'Well, that's great. Joey, will you sing another verse for Derek?'

Joey Feerick sang another verse of *The Meeting of the Waters* and Tom wondered what it was like having to spend all that time with the coats in the cloakroom, and the damp smell that was there on a wet day. Derek Birthistle had told him that on one occasion a lay sister brought him down to the kitchen and lifted him up on to a table so that he could watch the bread being made. Sometimes if they passed through the cloakroom the lay sisters would give him raisins or marzipan.

'There's a terrible old carry-on coming into the town, I hear,' Father Pierce said when the singing came to an end again and there was time to put in before the bell. 'I hope none of ye will be begging coppers to spend on the like of that.'

They knew he was joking. There was no one better than Father Pierce at pretending he was serious.

'Oh, I think coppers will be spent all right.' Sister Teresa Dolores, though patient and well liked, was not given to making jokes, or recognising them. 'When they could be saved for something sensible.'

The priest wagged his head deploringly, but was unable to control the smile that was wrenching his florid face in half. 'There's one boy I'm sure wouldn't be bothered with it. Isn't that right, Tom?'

'I'm going, Father.'

'Aren't you the holy terror, Tom!'

Derek Birthistle wasn't going to the knife-throwing. The day before he'd said his father wouldn't let him. Tom had watched the Protestant boy tightening his lips in disappointment when he'd confessed that. He went red in the face now, fearful in case Father Pierce asked him; he was ashamed because of his father.

'Well, that's great,' Father Pierce said instead, and he handed out sweets, one Rainbow Toffee each, to every member of the class. 'Ye're great scholars,' he said.

They all stood up to receive the sweets and remained

standing while the priest was still in the classroom because that was the practice. When he reached the door he turned as though he'd just remembered something, and surprised Tom by addressing him again. It was most unusual for a pupil to be addressed more than once in the same morning by Father Pierce.

'I hear they began work on the bridge,' he said. 'First thing they were at it, Tom.'

Tom hadn't known that, although he was aware of the talk there'd been about a bridge for the island, just as he'd been aware for so long of the talk about a tinned meat factory.

'I didn't know they'd started,' he said.

Father Pierce made his familiar gesture with his head, inclining it and wagging it at the same time. It would be a great easement for the island people, he said. It was a great decision that had been taken.

He left the classroom, not closing the door behind him. In the passage one of the senior girls rang the handbell, clanging it noisily the way that particular girl always did. The new bridge wouldn't make the journey from the gate-lodge easier. It would make it longer and more difficult because the bridge was being built where the water was narrowest, on the east side of the island, a much longer walk from the Carriglas gate-lodge than the walk to the pier. The ferry would cease as soon as the bridge was there, the ferryman said whenever the subject came up, adding that he'd be glad of an excuse to rest his bones.

'Are you looking after the well?' Sister Teresa Dolores asked, her eye picking Tom out as he began to leave the classroom. 'You're not forgetting it now?'

'I go there all right.'

'Stay beside it a long while when you're there. Touch the holy clay.'

He did stay a long while, Tom assured her, and he always touched the clay. Sister Teresa Dolores worried about things like that. She was always wanting to make sure that the rosary was being said and that the senior girls understood the requirements of Confession. There was worry in her eyes when she looked at you, and in the pull of her mouth, its corners drawn back into her face. She didn't want anyone to go to hell.

'Don't ever forget to go there, Tom.'

The well was at the ruined abbey on the island, where the saint had had his bed long before the abbey had been built to commemorate him. There was a slab of rock you could touch, which had been his pillow, and in a niche in the wall people left coins and rosary beads and crucifixes. You could put your hand down into the well and feel for the slightly moist clay. There wasn't any water in the well any more.

'I wouldn't ever forget,' Tom said.

He left the classroom and made his way to the Reverend Mother's house, where Sister Conheady had her library in an upstairs room. The journey was familiar to him; he made it twice a week. He rang the doorbell and then waited until a lay sister opened it and admitted him to the dark, silent hall, the linoleum on its floor sombrely gleaming. He waited in the room where the books were, all of them covered in brown paper by Sister Conheady and arranged on shelves in a glass-fronted bookcase. Hardly making a sound, except for the swish of her habit, Sister Conheady entered a moment later.

'Has she a couple to come back?' She unlocked a drawer in the bookcase, where details of the borrowing were kept. '*The Crescent Moon*, is it? And *Spring of Love*?'

Tom examined the handwritten titles on the brown-paper covers and thought they were probably that. 'Yes,' he said, handing Sister Conheady the books.

She was his favourite among the nuns. He considered her gentle, her pale face seeming delicate to him, her hands delicately thin. She reminded him of the picture of the glorified St Bernadette above the kitchen door in the gate-lodge. He couldn't imagine her ever being cross like Sister Sullivan always was or like his mother was sometimes. She didn't worry you with her eyes like Sister Teresa Dolores did, or not notice you like the Reverend Mother.

'I have this one for her,' Sister Conheady said.

She noted the title in a red exercise-book, taking her time because she was never in a hurry. She wrote with a pencil, and when she had finished she said she was sure the book would be enjoyed. 'Are they well across?' she enquired, and Tom said that as far as he knew the Rollestons were well.

It was the Rollestons who paid for Tom to attend the convent: his mother had told him that. Father Pierce had come over to the island specially. He had made the suggestion that in the circumstances it would be a good idea for Tom to go to the nuns until he was ready for the Christian Brothers. He had spoken to old Mrs Rolleston and apparently she had understood and had agreed. 'They're good to us, Tom,' his mother had said, and then had explained how she had been permitted to remain at Carriglas after his father's death, how Mrs Rolleston had insisted that she should move into the gate-lodge, abiding by the intention there had been. Everyone knew that his father's death had been an error. The Rollestons had endeavoured to make up for it.

'I'll be back maybe on Thursday,' he said to Sister Conheady. 'Or Wednesday if she'll have finished it.'

'I'm never far away, Tom.'

He always wished he could stay longer. A pleasant, shivery feeling sometimes ran through him when he was with Sister Conheady. It wasn't that he wanted to say anything in particular to her, or to listen to her saying something to him. It was just that being in her presence was nice.

*

John James made much the same journey as Tom had made in the early morning. When he stepped off the ferry barefoot children begged from him. Spring cabbages wilted beside turnips and carrots outside the small, poor shops of Narrow Lane. A smell of meal and porter wafted out of open doors. In the gutters there was a sludge of manure from last week's cattle and sheep fair.

He cashed a cheque in the Bank of Ireland, then strode the length of the town, out past the convent and the green railings of the Christian Brothers' school, on to the promenade. He wore a double-breasted flannel suit, his brown shoes shone, his tie and moustache shared a sprightliness. A yellow walking-stick almost disguised the hint of lameness in his gait that was a legacy of the war that had claimed his father.

Before turning into the Rose of Tralee boarding-house he paused and looked about him, his cigarette-case in one hand so that if necessary he might delay his progress beneath the pretext of selecting and nonchalantly lighting a cigarette. But since there was no one to be seen on the promenade he entered the boarding-house and made his way upstairs.

*

Carriglas, April 6th, 1931. It is the dead time of the afternoon between lunch and tea. Lionel is already back in the fields, his three sheepdogs keeping him company. Villana is out for her walk, Mrs Rolleston is resting, John James is visiting the woman he believes we do not know about. The house is always quiet during these afternoon hours – the time when the memories which govern me most persistently tug at my consciousness. I try not to think about the past, and urge myself to write instead that the daffodils bloomed a month ago, that quite soon there will be tulips and the first primroses and cowslips. It is I who arrange the flowers now, for Mrs Rolleston says it is too much for her, and Villana claims to be no good with flowers.

'You do not mind?' Villana said in a moment after lunch. 'You are not hurt by this?'

She meant by her forthcoming marriage, but why should I be hurt since in the meanwhile my brother has married someone else?

'Of course I am not hurt,' I replied. 'You know I wish you only happiness.'

She smiled gracefully, acknowledging that. They have at last begun to build the bridge, she remarked, and added that at least it would give employment. 'I dare say it's been a shock, coming back,' she added.

I smiled and shook my head, false in the implication. The avenue gates are now so streaked with green and rust that a camouflage has been formed, drawing them into landscape they once stood palely alien in. Grass is high on the avenue itself; weeds flourish in two rich channels on either side of it. The lawns that flank the house are only roughly cut, and the white paintwork of the hall-door and the windows is as marked and dirtied as the gates. In the drawing-room the chandeliers still hang grandly, the family portraits are as they've been before. But water, penetrating the wall of the French windows, has left a brown stain on the wallpaper; and the room is dingy. So, with similar discolouration, is the circular hall, and the empty alcoves of the green staircase wall seem less elegant than they were. Paint flakes away from windowsills. The nursery-schoolroom smells of the sun-scorched butterflies that have accumulated on its boarded floor.

When I wrote to Hugh to say I had returned to Carriglas he did not reply. In all the years that have gone by Hugh has never referred to the breaking off of the engagement, either in conversation on the few occasions when we've met, or in correspondence. Now that I have returned, I believe I may never hear from my brother again, and I do not know why.

*

Finnamore Balt wondered about the fate of his cat and his maid. The cat – resembling a white fluffball – had become so used to sitting on the wide windowsill of the hallway, between the lace curtains and the window-panes, that the deprivation of this simple pleasure seemed a cruelty. There was a certain haughtiness about the animal, disdain in the green eyes that observed the citizens of the town and the summer visitors passing to and fro all day long, yet it led a quiet life and did not deserve arbitrary punishment. 'I am really awfully sorry,' Villana had explained, 'but I cannot have a cat about me.' Finnamore's maid – a raw-boned woman who had been his parents' maid in their lifetime – was apparently not welcome at Carriglas either. 'I think,' he had replied with carefully judged energy as they stood waiting for the ferry the evening before, 'that is just a little unreasonable.' But Villana, smiling and slightly shaking her head, had been reluctant to pursue the conversation.

In his office, among mahogany filing-cabinets and stacks of books recording legal precedent, Finnamore Balt sighed. He could not think what he might possibly say to his maid, who'd been loyal for so long; he could think of no home for a cat that had been, and still was, a comfort to him. These thoughts were interrupted by knuckles rapping discreetly on a panel of the door; when he called out, his clerk entered with a document he had asked him to find. Eugene Prille was oval-shaped, no taller than a child and with a child's complexion, yet was sagacious to a degree. Finnamore knew that before the week was out he would consult him about his twin worries. He would continue to wrestle with them himself, he would lose sleep over them, he would again bring them up at Carriglas, but in the end it would fall to Eugene Prille to provide a solution.

'Thank you, Eugene,' he said, grateful in another connection. 'You have been swift over that.'

'There were but two places to search, Mr Balt.'

The clerk soundlessly retreated; Finnamore returned to

his meditations. Marriage was bound to bring awkwardness; you could not expect otherwise, especially when one of the parties was set in his ways, and that he himself was he did not deny for a moment. Human nature was human nature, as changeable and extraordinary as all the landscape of the world might seem if encompassed and contained in one single lump. A solicitor saw human nature in such miraculous variety, and if there was a single conclusion to be reached it was that in matters governed by human vagaries and weaknesses the law could not be dispensed with. Disputes concerning boundaries and the ownership of land, concerning inheritance and agreements entered into without a solicitor's advice, concerning breach of promise, slanderous statements, imputations, the casting of aspersions, legacies, mortgages, wandering animals, concerning the realm of bankruptcy, the realm of leases and rents, the drawing up of wills, the proving of wills, the questioning of wills – all threaded their way back to vagaries and weaknesses. For five generations Harbinson and Balt, in these same offices, had stood by victim or miscreant, wielding the letter of the law as their single weapon.

As was proper in a solicitor, Finnamore revered the law. Through the law he looked out at the world, judged greed and foolishness and decency and wisdom. The law it was that allowed him his knowledge of the neighbourhood he lived in, and its people: family histories and family origins filled the mahogany filing-cabinets, filled drawers and desks and forgotten deed boxes. Changes in fortune, decline, decay, the journey into exile, rescue by dowry, wealth lost or wealth regained: in documents that were browning or pristine fresh such human variation was recorded in language that Finnamore, after nearly forty years' experience, no longer found difficult. That the Ganters of Boherboy were the cousins of the Uniaches of Enniskeen, that the Clonmel Breretons were attached to the Charleville Frenches, that the Nallens had too often married the

Knightlys, was random fruit from an orchard of genealogical trees. The Rollestons' connection with the Pollexfens, and with the Camiers and the Ennises, was present in Finnamore's office; and even, passingly, the fact that the Rollestons, arriving in the wake of Oliver Cromwell, had dispossessed the Cantillons of their island and sent them on their way to the stony wilderness of Mayo. Big houses and small farms rubbed shoulders in the drawers and cabinets of Harbinson and Balt; the past lay down with what the present offered.

Yet, aware as he was of the humanity that fed his profession, and the facts it threw up for his scrutiny, Finnamore had all his life failed to perceive it clearly. He did not understand it as he understood the law. He recognised its crude mass; he treated it with respect, since he also sensed its power. But neither in himself nor in others did he appreciate mystery and subtlety, or the grey shadows of contradiction, or unreason. The world he looked out at was positive and negative, black and white.

In spite of this, or perhaps because of it, Finnamore lived with a dream. It had been part of him since he was a younger man, just turned twenty-nine. 'You'll need to attend to that in person,' his father had said. 'It's what they like.' And for the first time Finnamore had made the journey to Carriglas, to draw up an agreement about the selling of a larch wood. Villana, still a child, had enchanted him in a way he would not have believed possible. He had never found himself drawn towards the Protestant girls he met at parties in the neighbourhood, or the Catholic girls of the shops; he had been conscious of no desire. But he returned from Carriglas that day feeling elated and light-headed, and in church on Sundays his eyes afterwards strayed endlessly to the fair-haired child. His dream began then: it was that his own advice and expertise should be responsible for restoring the family fortunes of the Rollestons, and the Carriglas estate, to their former grandeur. It did not for a second occur to him that one day he might find himself marrying Villana Rolleston, only that, in his work, he might often visit the family and that she would be there. He learnt the house's history and related it in the Rollestons' drawing-room, for they did not appear to be fully familiar with it. He told them how the house had been built on the site of the Cantillons' castle when the first Rollestons grew tired of living in the castle itself, how the stone had been re-cut and dressed by Jeremiah O'Toole of Cork, how an Italian called Martelli, of Dublin, had been commissioned for the plasterwork of the dining-room and the inner hall. Bars had been incorporated in the nursery windows at the wish of the wife of the John Rolleston of that particular time. The architect who'd decided on concave walls and had created so spectacular an effect with the French windows of the southern façade had been a Mr Forbes, and he it was who had also designed the Carriglas gardens. In the drawing-room Finnamore spoke of a Rolleston of the eighteenth century who had attempted to grow bananas in the conservatory, and of a later Rolleston who had attempted to swim to the next island, no more than a rock, along the coast. A bonfire had burned all night among the standing stones, celebrating the victory at Waterloo. He spoke of another John Rolleston, who had married Catherine Esmond of Ninemilecross, the couple later known as the Famine Rollestons because of their compassion at that time. As best they could, they found work for their tenants so that they might be protected from starvation by being paid in kind. The Carriglas gardens were kept up as never before; more stabling was built; a second avenue, long since grown over, was surfaced; the cliff walk round the island was cleared. The big pier was built at that time, but still some kind of guilt persisted in John and Catherine Rolleston. The famine had scattered death and suffering so generously that even after the new potato crop succeeded the survivors on the island spoke of walking to the exile ships of Cork. The hunger there had been, pressing hard upon centuries of poverty, had left them without heart, and it was then that the Rollestons waived their rents and their tithes in favour of the families who remained. John Rolleston was convinced that this reduction in the estate's income could somehow be made up in other ways. 'Unhappily,' Finnamore had reminded his listeners in the drawing-room, 'he was wrong.'

That was the crux of it. The waived monies had never been collected since, title to land had been lost through neglect. For nearly twenty years Finnamore had been studying precedents in other parts of the country, testing his arguments with all the legal vigour he possessed, establishing that their strength would hold in a court of law. No suit must be lost once it was entered upon; it was unthinkable that the Rollestons should end up with only the expense of failure. 'Haste is the enemy,' he had said more than once in the drawing-room.

Finnamore had not experienced jealousy when, in the midst of all this, Villana became engaged to Hugh Pollexfen – only distressed that Hugh Pollexfen might take her away from Carriglas. Hugh Pollexfen was an army officer, as her father had been and as John James at one time had aspired to be; but as a suitor, he possessed no property, being the son of a penurious clergyman. After the first anxious months of that engagement it became clear that because of these circumstances Villana's husband would not be taking her far, since there was nowhere to take her to. Rather, it seemed, Hugh Pollexfen would join the family at Carriglas, and help to farm the land.

In his office, which was a place of consolation and tranquillity, Finnamore recalled how he had envisaged the future. He had thought to admire Villana's beauty from a distance, she married to the man she had chosen, he himself still visiting the drawing-room to talk about the family and the house. More times than he could count, he had observed the Sunday procession of the Rollestons from the quays to church: the old woman walking slowly between her two sons, John James smartly turned out, Lionel not at all so, Villana coming a little behind them. But it was Sarah Pollexfen, not her brother, who had returned to walk with them now, opening an umbrella when it rained. 'We might issue seizures,' he had pressed in the drawing-room a year ago, but to his considerable astonishment he had received no encouragement. 'You must come more often,' Villana said instead, having invited him to accompany her on a walk. Later their conversations acquired a different form. 'I am not the marrying kind,' he honestly pointed out, knowing he was not. 'And yet you love me,' she replied. 'You have loved me for all my life nearly.' Never once had he guessed she knew. 'Marriage would not mean children,' she had softly promised, as if to reassure him. 'I do not wish for children, Finny.'

*

Four o'clock struck in the inner hall, a disturbance heralded by mechanical wheezing and followed by the lingering echo of vibration. Mrs Rolleston heard the sounds in the conservatory and was pleased: she took pride in the fact that neither her hearing nor her sight had deteriorated to an uncomfortable degree. She had been thinking that the conservatory could do with a coat of paint and wondering if Mr Keevan would have to come over from the town.

'There's tea,' Villana called out from the door that led to the house. She was dressed in green, a tweed skirt and blouse, a cameo brooch at her throat. When she spoke she did not raise her voice but projected it through the warm foliage, over pots and ornamental urns. Her looks were certainly striking now, Mrs Rolleston reflected, her skin like porcelain, her pale hair silky, her eyes as they had ever been.

'It has suddenly occurred to me, Villana, that they will

say you are marrying for money. No doubt they are saying it already.'

They walked together to the drawing-room. Tea and madeira cake were on a table close to where Villana sat. She poured two cups and cut two slices.

'In fact, it isn't true.' Villana shook her head, lending emphasis to her denial and then dismissing the suspicions by advancing the conversation in a different direction. 'There is something more to the point,' she said, and went on to reveal that she had at last been permitted to reject the house near the promenade which her fiancé had inherited on his parents' death.

'So Finnamore will live among us?'

'I am suggesting it.'

Mrs Rolleston's query had been vague; she was thinking of something else. If the regiment had not rejected Lionel as unfit for the war he would not have come back, or else would have come back more knocked about than his brother. She knew that in her bones: it was the bright side. She had lost a son and a husband in foolish wars but at least her grandsons had been spared, with only a shattered leg between them. Hugh, of course, had come back also. Hugh had apparently married a girl in Colchester, wherever that was.

'Finny will pay something,' Villana said. 'That's only fair.' She knocked a cigarette from a packet with a black cat on it. 'The wedding date we thought of is towards the end of August, Grandmamma.' She lit the cigarette. 'The twenty-sixth. A Wednesday.'

'I see.'

She had known Finnamore Balt for a lifetime and had never in all those years guessed that his uncomfortable hatchet of a face would one day come to be there at every mealtime. Villana didn't love him any more than John James loved his promenade woman or Lionel loved anyone at all. *You never tell me how your grandchildren are getting*

(45)

on these days: the post that morning had brought the letter she had wondered about when she first awoke. *I often think about your grandchildren. I wish you'd tell me*, the looped handwriting had chided.

'And then we are to honeymoon at the Killarney lakes.'

More tea was poured. Once she had been to the Killarney lakes herself. Famous poets had apparently been inspired there. The surrounding mountains echoed strangely.

'Finny is kind, you know.'

'I did not think otherwise. Am I confused, or is there dance music playing somewhere?'

'Actually there is.' Villana had heard the music on her walk, drifting over from the town. She'd remarked on it to Mrs Haverty, who'd said that a couple calling themselves the Zodiacs had arrived in the town that morning, a man who threw knives at his wife. Mrs Haverty had explained that you could hear the music because it was being relayed through a loudspeaker as an advertisement for the entertainment.

'I wonder it's allowed,' Mrs Rolleston said.

'Well, I've told you, Grandmamma,' Villana concluded. 'And now I'm going to tell Lionel. If anyone objects to Finny coming here it has only to be said.' She gathered up her cigarettes and lighter, and her novel from the convent library. 'Would Miss Laffey make something for me?' She turned to her grandmother before she left the drawing-room. 'Nothing frilly, quite without elaboration. Miss Laffey should be up to that. Shall I write a note for Brigid's child to take?'

'If that seems appropriate to you.'

'I shall not have bridesmaids.'

Soon after Villana's departure from the drawing-room Mrs Rolleston made her way to the kitchen. The letter was in the drawer of her dressing-table, the stamp fitted as snugly as possible into the envelope's corner, the two ruled lines beneath the careful *Private*. She carried the image with her to the kitchen, and thankfully lost it when another conversation began.

'The beef's poor, ma'am,' Brigid complained. 'Broderick's sending over scandalous stuff these days.' As she spoke she lifted a web of suet from the offending joint and exposed the meat's shortcomings to the old woman's gaze. 'Neither hung nor lean, ma'am. I've put it to Miss Pollexfen.'

Mrs Rolleston nodded. She tried to think about the meat, but found herself dwelling instead on the fact that one of the kitchen windows was slightly open. There'd been a time when these windows were always kept closed because of flies and bluebottles. The men would unharness the carts in the yard and then the horses would be led to the paddock, leaving the flies behind.

'What's the matter with Broderick?' she said, making an effort. 'Is he drinking?'

She still liked coming down to the kitchen. In a way she liked it better than poking about the conservatory, or being in the drawing-room or dining-room. The kitchen was somehow more a place to linger in, or had become so. The vast oak dresser, standing an inch or so free of a pink-distempered surface, was reassuring. Sometimes, in the middle of the night, she would wonder if it was still there and then go down to make certain that it was, not later revealing to anyone the doubt she'd been subjected to. Alone in the kitchen's spaciousness, she would admire the windows and wall-cupboards that so gracefully accommodated the faint concavity of the walls. The range and the long, scrubbed table formed a trinity with the dresser, the range the kitchen's heart, as the kitchen was the household's. When she stood there in the night that was how she thought of it.

'I hadn't heard he was drinking, ma'am,' Brigid said.

Whenever his wife became pregnant Broderick haunted

the public houses. He was a man brought low by small misfortunes.

'Ask Miss Pollexfen to send over a note,' she advised. 'Ask if he could manage an improvement.'

The new maid, Patty, freckles all over her cheeks and nose and forehead, incredulous about the eyes, sat at the long table in her afternoon black, her lace-trimmed cap and apron crisply white. Mrs Rolleston's arrival had caused her to rise to her feet, but she had been motioned to sit down again. Her broad, plump hands were still awkward with cutlery and plates, her brown hair forever escaping from the pins that tugged it into place beneath her cap. She would never learn, she had privately confided to Brigid, but Brigid told her not to sound like a fool.

Mrs Rolleston watched while the unsatisfactory beef was placed in the oven. 'There's potatoes in the scullery that want skinning,' Brigid said, sharply, to the maid. 'And carrots that want cleaning with a scrubbing-brush. Take off that apron and put on an overall.'

Patty rose in a hurry to do as she was bidden. Mrs Rolleston lingered, and when the sound of running water began in the distant scullery she said:

'Is that child content, Brigid?'

'Why wouldn't she be, ma'am? Isn't it a great chance for her?'

'Has she stopped crying, though? Is she lonesome still?'

Brigid sniffed. She folded her arms, on which the sleeves of the jumper she wore beneath her overall were rolled up beyond her elbows. The girl was best kept busy, she declared. When a girl like that was cutting kindling or skimming milk, where was the time for tears?

'Keep an eye on her all the same, Brigid. It isn't easy for the young ones sometimes.'

As she left the kitchen, she realised that that was why she had paid the visit: she had been worried about the new maid because she was so young. Some time or other, perhaps yesterday or the day before, she had woken out of a dream, feeling sorry for somebody and knowing it was Patty. She'd been sorry for the others too, all the new girls who had come to Carriglas, only fifteen or sixteen years old most of them. 'God, ma'am, it's a great house you have,' Kathleen Quigley had said, and she, too, had been lonesome. 'It's only I miss the fields, ma'am,' Kathleen Quigley had said. 'It's only I miss the ways we have at home.'

Brigid followed Patty to the scullery and worked beside her at the draining-board, peeling apples for a charlotte. She had become used over the years to Mrs Rolleston's tenderness, indeed she had benefited from it herself, but she often reflected that what the old woman didn't realise, and never would, was that compassion was sometimes inappropriately extended. Girls like this raw creature beside her knew better where they were with regular scolding. Concern for their well-being only led to confusion, and then the bouts of weeping began.

'Did you hear the music Mrs Haverty was on about?' she enquired with a briskness she considered suitable.

Patty shook her head again. No music had penetrated to the depths of the kitchen quarters and, unlike Brigid, she had not been out in the yard. She hadn't understood the information imparted by Mrs Haverty about the entertainment, but she brushed the clay from another carrot before she asked about it. Brigid said:

'He has a woman standing up against a board and then he pitches knives at her. He has twenty knives stuck into the board before he's finished.'

'Glory be to God, are you serious, Brigid?' Scrubbing-brush and carrot dropped into the sink. Open-mouthed, her jaw slackened to its extent, Patty stared at her kitchen superior.

'If you could see yourself,' Brigid sharply admonished her. 'Don't look like a fool, girl.'

'But isn't it shocking all the same? Wouldn't you think she'd get cut?'

'Get on with your work, girl.'

On the way upstairs Mrs Rolleston's train of thought continued. The memory of Kathleen Quigley became the memory of Haverty saying, 'I haven't told Brigid.' Just for a moment she had closed her eyes and then had gone to the kitchen to tell Brigid herself, while Haverty and another man gathered up the remains of the body on the avenue. Mrs Haverty had stayed in the kitchen because she'd asked her to and she'd gone herself to the pier. She'd waited there through a night that never became dark and saw them as the birds began to sing — Hugh and her grandsons rowing the boat they had earlier rowed across to the party, four uniforms in a second boat, a third one trailing behind. She heard their laughter and their voices becoming louder. There were other girls besides Villana: people had been invited to breakfast at Carriglas. *If you persist in fraternising with the barracks*, a message received a week ago had threatened, *measures will be taken*. Villana had laughed.

She entered her bedroom and pulled open the drawer of her dressing-table. She took the letter to the chair by the window. When she'd told them they had remained as they were, arrested in their movements, a girl about to step out of a boat, John James and Lionel already on the pier. One of the other men swore. 'We can guess who our visitor was,' she'd said before she walked away.

Fifteen shillings would see me right, she read.

*

She spoke from her afternoon bed, paying him a compliment, saying he was her king. He, naked by the window though obscured from the promenade by double net curtains, lit a cigarette. She preferred him not to smoke when he lay beside her, and so obligingly he rose when the moment for a cigarette arrived.

'Darling, you're cross about that bridge.'

He shook his head, then changed his mind and said the bridge was inconveniently placed. No proper thought had been given to the matter.

'A conveyance'll be necessary, pet. You'll need a motor-car.'

'I have no money for a motor-car.'

'Come back into bed, honey, and warm me up.'

The boarding-house proprietress's bedroom had pink, striped wallpaper on its walls, with bunches of pinkish lilies cascading in each corner and running along in a frieze below the picture rail. There was a wash-stand with a basin and jug on it, and a large wardrobe and a table with a mirror propped against a vase, in front of which Mrs Moledy's cosmetics, hairpins and other aids to beauty were laid out. A crucifix hung between the curtained windows, and on the floor beneath it a rubber plant stood in a brass container. Sacred statues elsewhere adorned the room. At the foot of the bed were the two chairs on which Mrs Moledy laid her clothes when she divested herself of them.

'Come on, my honey,' she urged again. Her fleshy, powdered face simpered from the pillows, her double chin bunched into pale folds. Mrs Moledy had been widowed for seven years and John James's friend for five. Her bulk beneath the sheet and blankets was considerable, by chance reflecting the appetite of her passion. 'I would advance you the money for a motor-car,' she offered when she had settled his limbs about her pin-cushion plumpness. An arrangement could easily be drawn up: it was not unusual for a woman in her position to lend money. Her fingers, as she spoke, explored the flesh of her companion. They traced the outline of his ribs, loitering on his stomach. They touched his region of reproduction. 'Oh, you are my king!' she murmured.

The boarding-house on that April afternoon was quiet. Its two permanent lodgers were at work and it was too early by a month or so for the first of its seasonal visitors. Mrs Moledy's maid was given Monday afternoons off.

'King!' Mrs Moledy suddenly cried out. 'King of my castle!'

She dozed, and he thought how much he disliked her. Five years ago, one warm midday, he had been sitting on a seat on the promenade, watching the fishing boats returning one by one. She had addressed him by name, had walked by, and on her way back had sat down beside him. Afterwards she confessed that she'd seen him from the boarding-house and had come out specially. She played him a record on her gramophone. 'Get along, little doggy,' a tinny voice had sung. 'Get along, get along.'

Beside him, she awoke. Her mood had changed, as it often did in the course of an afternoon. He recognised even before she spoke the mood he disliked most of all.

'Oh, I would love it if we could go to a show like that!' She pouted. She protruded her lower lip beyond the upper one. She sniffed, as if tearful. She wasn't good enough, she supposed.

'It isn't that at all.'

'It's always no with you, darling.'

John James, drawing upon his experience of the relationship, tightened his face and remained silent.

'I thought you might say yes for once, darling.'

It was always best to keep as quiet as possible, not to argue. Last week she'd mentioned the entertainment that was advertised, some dreadful kind of circus sideshow. She'd hinted at first, not making much of the possibility, which was always her way. Now she was suggesting that they should walk together along the promenade, with the whole town watching, in order to attend it.

'No,' he repeated, and he tried to think of other times in his life, of being at school, of conversations with his father. Had his father, widowed all those years, visited a Catholic woman somewhere? Had he, too, experienced the torment of remorse and resolved never to return? It was hard to imagine his father suffering like that. It was hard to imagine his father in the company of such a woman, black hair sprouting from her armpits. His father had gone to his death thinking the world of him, the eldest of his children, and his inheritor: John James believed that.

'You'd hate the whole thing,' he forced himself to say. 'Some poor woman within a hair's breadth of her death.'

But Mrs Moledy protested that she would enjoy the entertainment like any other person would. She had no life, waiting from one week to the next, everything underhand. Declare to God, she stated, she only felt herself when she was confessing her sins. 'This one the worst of them,' she said.

'You're not telling me you let on about this at your Confessions?'

Sulkily, she did not reply. But when he repeated the question his tone of voice betrayed his alarm. Pleased, she said:

'It's a mortal sin, pet. I have to arrange redemption.'

'Redemption?'

'I have to atone, darling. Penance and forgiveness: you don't have it in your church.'

'Which priest do you go to?'

'It's not like that, darling. It's different than going to a doctor. Usually, though, it's Father Pierce.'

He could sense her enjoying herself. He could sense her punishing him. I will not return to this room, he said to himself. Next Monday she can lie there with her powder on her and cry her bloody liver out.

'No need to fret, darling. Father Pierce hears all sorts.'

'My God!'

He rose from the bed, the floor cold on the soles of his feet. He remembered his father going to Dublin on his own, remaining for a few days in Davison's Hotel: he wondered again about a woman. Sometimes on their way back from school in Shropshire he and Lionel would spend a night in Davison's, all of it arranged for them. He remembered Barmy Jessop claiming he'd gone with a woman of the streets, and wondering himself if such women were to be found in Dublin. He and Barmy Jessop and Asquith-Jones used to talk about things like that. He remembered how the three of them had drunk communion wine with the night-watchman in his boiler room, and how Barmy Jessop had rung the Chapel bell in the middle of the night, raising a fire alarm.

'Darling, I'm only codding you.' She giggled from the pillows. 'Come on back in.'

She swore it wasn't true. She made him take the statue of the Virgin from the shelf on the wall and he held it while she swore. 'Janey Mack!' she exclaimed, laughing. 'If anyone could see us!'

She attempted more cajoling, but he said it was time to go. He fiddled with his studs and cufflinks, hurrying to get them into place, knowing her good mood wouldn't last. He could sense her searching her mind for some new shaft of attack.

'One of the boarders'll take me,' she finally threatened. 'We'll make an evening of it.' She mentioned Myley Flynn's public house, saying an hour or so would probably be spent there. 'You'd never know what would happen on a night like that,' she casually remarked, 'with everyone excited by the show.'

*

Villana stood in the ice-house, where Hugh Pollexfen had first kissed her. No longer used for any purpose, grimy and cobwebbed, the ice-house had been their secret place. A brick ledge ran round the walls, almost a bench. You could sit on it, crouching beneath the first of the grey marble shelves that ran from wall to wall also. The first time she and Hugh had found privacy in the ice-house they had not sat down, but on subsequent occasions they had huddled together in a corner, their arms around one another. 'Oh, Hugh,' she murmured now, wondering what he was doing at this moment. She did not know the name of the girl he had married because she had never wanted to, nor the names of his children, of which there were three. England was not a place she would care to find herself in, formal and polite, its landscape said to be like that also. She had never been there but could easily guess. At this moment his wife was perhaps calling him into whatever house they lived in, where the children would be primly waiting around a tea table. 'Hugh,' she murmured again. 'Oh, Hugh, how ridiculous!'

*

Ploughing, Lionel walked patiently, the horse's weariness at the end of the day dictating their shared pace. Almost as tall and thin as his father had been, a little stooped even though he was only a few years into his thirties, Lionel at a distance presented the impression of wiry strength: seen closer, the cast of his face suggested vulnerability, as it had in childhood. He was aware of his brother's liaison with the boarding-house keeper but did not ever think about it. He was bewildered by his sister's forthcoming marriage and by the fact, an hour ago revealed to him, that her husband was to live at Carriglas. He regretted the building of the bridge, but what concerned him more were the crops he sowed, and his animals, and the trees on the skyline. That was his life.

The evening sun, slanting across the furrows, caught for an instant the blade of the plough. Some distance away Lionel's three sheepdogs, crouched around an open gate, suggested protection, although he in no way required it. They were dogs who disdained the attentions, and the commands, of others; they followed him wherever he went. He called them now, and they came to him swiftly. 'Good girl, good girl,' he murmured to the horse, releasing it of its burden and leading it from the field.

*

On the ferryboat Haverty and the ferryman talked about racehorses. The Gullet had failed, making it three times in a row. Market Rasen was mentioned, and Towcester and Aintree, which Tom at first assumed to be the names of other horses and then realised were English race-courses. Butt Nolan was advising Persian Prince, the ferryman said.

'I have to go down the town first,' Haverty revealed when he and Tom stepped on to the quay. 'I have five minutes of business.'

So they turned to the right when they came to South Main Street, and entered Spillane's public house at the bottom of Michael Davitt Hill. 'Lemonade and biscuits for the boy,' Haverty ordered, having also delivered his own requirement. Tom had never been in a public house before although he had once or twice been in the grocery attached to one. Often when something his mother wanted for cooking wasn't available in Meath's or Dungan's or the London and Newcastle he had to try in other places, usually unsuccessfully. Very little had ever been available in Spillane's grocery, no rashers because there wasn't a bacon machine, no jams or jellies, no packets of peas or cornflour. But in the bar lemonade and biscuits were supplied without difficulty.

Men were standing at the counter, leaning their elbows on it; a few were sitting at tables. Mr Coyne, of the garage, was there; and Mr O'Hagan from the post office. There were other men whom Tom did not recognise. The exterior of Spillane's — its blue paintwork and the raised marbled letters that spelt out its title, the advertisements for tea and Bisto in one window, whiskey and porter in the other — suggested a greater promise than either grocery or bar fulfilled. A murkiness prevailed in the latter, and its occu-

(56)

pants as a result had acquired the nature of shadows. Exposed to the daylight, those men whom Tom did not recognise might have at once become familiar.

Mr O'Hagan, seated with Mr Coyne, spoke to Haverty about the racehorse called The Gullet. Butt Nolan deserved hanging, he said. Butt Nolan had sold him inside information for the usual consideration, the result of which being he'd placed money on an animal that had difficulty in walking let alone winning a race. The skin of Mr O'Hagan's face was white, his pale moustache was lank; he wore wire-rimmed spectacles, behind which his eyes were melancholy. Mr Coyne had a stomach that protruded, a gleaming bald head and a small moustache. His eyes were like two rosary beads, so minute that they disappeared into the fat of his face when he laughed or frowned. He had eleven children, all of them girls. Mr O'Hagan was a bachelor.

'Persian Prince's your man,' Haverty said. He drew a hand across his face, wiping away froth left behind by his stout. 'John Joe Shevlin up. Unbeatable.'

'No better man,' Mr Coyne contributed.

'He has England defeated.'

'I would agree with that.'

But Mr O'Hagan gloomily shook his head. If Butt Nolan advised Persian Prince he wouldn't touch the animal with a pole, John Joe Shevlin notwithstanding. 'Another two bob gone west on The Gullet. Does Nolan think they grow in the woods?'

No reply was offered. If there was a young fellow that ever sat on a horse with the skill of John Joe, Haverty continued, he had yet to be shown him. All animals acquired quality under John Joe.

'I would agree with that,' said Mr Coyne.

Other horses were mentioned, Happy Honeymoon and Fancy Cottage, and other jockeys. Haverty ceased to wipe the froth from around his mouth. Mr Coyne whistled for a moment beneath his breath. 'All I'm saying,' said Mr

O'Hagan, 'is Butt Nolan's a chancer. I've nothing against young Shevlin.'

In his mouth the lemonade turned the biscuits into a sweet mush which Tom held there for as long as he could. It surprised him that the men remained where they were instead of going to see the knife-throwing. You could hear the music from it on the quays and in South Main Street, much louder than it had been on the island. The ferryman said the entire town was going to it.

'I'm not saying for a moment,' Mr O'Hagan lugubriously persisted, 'that Persian Prince isn't a well-bred animal. I'm not saying that at all.'

'Wasn't he bred in Tipperary? Amn't I right in that?' Mr Coyne enquired.

Haverty said he was. Born and bred in Tipperary, as fine a young horse as ever left the county. A horse you'd like to see doing well.

'I have nothing against the horse,' insisted Mr O'Hagan. 'I'm not saying I have.'

'Ah sure, we know you haven't.' To Tom's dismay Mr Coyne rapped on the pebbly glass between the bar and the grocery and called out an order for further refreshment. 'Another lemonade for the boy,' he instructed, drawing from his glass the dregs of its black liquid. Watching this, Tom felt uneasy in his stomach because the smell the stout gave off made him think that something in it had gone bad. Haverty and Mr O'Hagan drained their glasses also.

'John Joe's from Carlow,' Mr Coyne stated when the freshly poured drinks were placed on the table. 'Amn't I right in that?'

Haverty said he believed that was so. A credit to Carlow, he said. And wasn't the young horse a credit to Tipp?

'Oh, credit certainly. Credit where credit's due.'

Mr O'Hagan noisily sniffed. 'I have nothing against either horse or jockey. I have no bone to pick over either of them.' He drew his breath in, holding it for a moment or two before slowly releasing it. Sometimes Tom had to buy a postal order for Mrs Rolleston from him and when he asked for it Mr O'Hagan did exactly the same thing, delaying the release of his breath for as long as he could, and only reaching for the box where he kept the postal orders when no further sound came from his nose.

'Will it still be going?' Tom asked.

None of the men replied. Mr O'Hagan repeated what he had several times repeated already in connection with Butt Nolan. Mr Coyne said John Joe Shevlin's father was a man who knew his onions, the way he'd got John Joe into a stables when he was five years old. It was a story he'd heard, and he didn't doubt a word of it. Haverty said a Carlow man always knew his onions.

'Will the knife-throwing still be going? Will we be late for it?'

Haverty blinked. He pursed his lips in deliberation and for a moment his lean countenance seemed leaner. True enough, if they were late they could have trouble getting back across the water. They could run into difficulties because your man might be cantankerous about obliging them with the ferryboat.

'Wait till you'll have your bridge,' said Mr Coyne.

But Haverty said they'd have to wait a while yet. He leaned across the table with a smile of amusement on his face. He suggested there'd be hard words all round if he remained in Spillane's until the bridge was completed, although for himself he wouldn't mind. He laughed noisily and so did Mr Coyne. Mr O'Hagan said that if Butt Nolan came into the public house he'd give him the sharp department of his tongue.

'Are they pleased across about the bridge?' Mr Coyne enquired when the laughter had calmed down.

Haverty shook his head. 'How would they be? Isn't it the wrong side for all of us?'

'I know what you mean.'

'Listen to me,' Haverty said to Tom. 'I have business I haven't finished with Mr Coyne and Mr O'Hagan. Go on up yourself and see what's doing and come down to the quays after it's done. I'll be waiting by the boat for you.'

'The Zodiacs is famous the length and breadth of Ireland,' Mr Coyne remarked. 'When they've done their stuff throw them that.' He gave Tom a ha'penny, and it struck Tom as odd that Mr Coyne should pay money for what he did not intend to witness. He accepted the coin, saying he would pass it on.

'Don't be long now,' Haverty said. 'Don't have me waiting all night on the quays.'

Tom hurried in South Main Street, past familiar windows and doorways. 'Hey, mister,' Humpy Geehan shouted out at him from the steps of Lett's Arcade. 'How're you, Humpy?' he called back, which was how he'd heard other boys replying to the greeting. A cluster of bicycles leaned against Morrissy's windowsills, a horse and cart was tied to a lamp-post outside Myley Flynn's. People crowded into the confectioner's and tobacconist's before going on to the knife-throwing. Two dogs fought in the middle of the street. A girl was waiting outside Traynor's Picture Palace.

Beyond South Main Street the houses became taller. Brass plates indicated the services of Surgeon Woulfe and K. J. Ikely, B. Dent., of doctors, and solicitors who were also commissioners for oaths. Crowds hurried on the promenade, a bustling movement surging in the direction of the Zodiacs' music. *World's Most Dangerous Act!* fresh posters proclaimed. *Regularly Performed Before Royalty!* They were stuck on to the promenade lamp-posts and the telegraph poles and the sides of the bandstand; they decorated the flaking yellow walls of a billiard-hall where nobody played billiards any more.

'Is it Tom?' someone behind him said, and he knew without turning round that it was Holy Mullihan. 'Are you out on your own, Tom?'

There was no reason why Tom should have been frightened of Holy Mullihan, for he was not a bully, indeed rather the opposite. It was just that there was something about him, something in his manner and his way, that caused apprehension when his company continued for too long. Holy Mullihan had a widow's peak and soft dark hair on his upper lip. His wrists protruded from the frayed cuffs of a black jacket, and the ends of his trousers scarcely reached his boots. His black tie was tightly knotted within a soiled collar; his Adam's apple bobbed noticeably in a scrawny neck. Holy Mullihan was never seen in the company of the boys who were his own age at the Christian Brothers', preferring to draw younger boys aside in order to conduct conversations with them about religious matters. He had already declared his intention of entering the priesthood.

'Will we go together, Tom?' he suggested now. 'Isn't it great to see the people out enjoying themselves?'

'Will we be late?'

'As long as there's people to watch, the entertainment will go on. It's a hard way to make a living, Tom.'

In his excitement Tom didn't mind the company of Holy Mullihan, although normally he would have tried to get away from him. The music was now so loud that conversation in any case was difficult. You had to shout, the way you had to on the ferry, and Holy Mullihan's voice was always kept very low, hardly more than a whisper. He had raised it in order to say what he'd said already, but as they walked together on the promenade he didn't say anything else.

The knife-throwing act took place on a piece of land donated by a man who had years ago left the town and become a candy king in America. A park was to be created there, to be called after Father Ignatius Quirke, a temperance leader of the past; but the money that was to pay for all this, and for a statue of the priest, had never arrived, and the town was left with a gift of derelict land only. Every year Duffy's Circus set up its marquees there; so did Toft's Roundabouts and Bumper Cars.

A string of electric lights, high above the heads of the gathering crowd, now formed an illuminated rectangle on this wasteland. Within it stood a green van, close to which was a timber door attached to two posts driven into the ground. The back of the van was obscured by yellow curtains draped over a wire that ran around four similar posts, from one of which hung the Zodiacs' loudspeaker. '... *She is far from the land where her young hero sleeps,*' a tenor voice plaintively whined. '*And lovers are round her, sighing ...*'

Abruptly the music ceased. A woman in a red bathing dress emerged from the curtains at the back of the van and took up a position against the door. A man tied a red handkerchief around her eyes. He pushed her back against the door so that she was touching it. Then he disappeared into the yellow curtains and when he came out he was carrying his knives. He was a hollow-faced man in shirt-sleeves, wearing neither collar nor tie and with a scar down the left side of his face. He held his arms out, brandishing six knives in either hand. It was a demand for attention, and when the talking did not cease he shouted out that he could not perform until the silence was total. Muttering and laughter dribbled and broke off. 'A single flaw in this act,' the man shouted, 'and that beautiful lady will be deprived of life.' When the gasp that succeeded this claim had subsided he took up his position, and then carefully laid the twelve knives in a row on the ground in front of him. 'The Zodiacs have performed before royalty,' he reminded his audience, 'in four contingents. The Zodiacs, ladies and gentlemen, are strangers to fear.' While he spoke the blindfolded woman bared her teeth in a laughing smile. At a command from her companion she became still and one by one the knives thudded into the door around her. When all twelve were embedded in the timber she stepped forward and turned round and round, still smiling and with her arms held up, to show that no blood had been drawn. Her companion gestured towards the door, drawing attention to the outline of her body depicted by the knives, which he then pulled out. When he had done so the woman again took up her position. He spread sheets of newspaper over her, attaching them swiftly to the door with thumb-tacks. Again the knives flashed through the air and when the last one had been thrown the woman stepped forward as she had before, bursting out of the newspaper. 'Next you will witness an act,' the man announced, drawing out the knives and bundling away the newspaper, 'never before performed. Tonight, ladies and gentlemen, we offer you the skill of the most daring knife-throwing act in the world.' This time it was he who tied the handkerchief over his eyes. Two girls screamed. The woman kept her smile in place while the knives struck the timber around her. Tom didn't look.

Shouting and whistling caused him to open his eyes again. Coins were thrown on to the ground and the man and the woman bent to pick them up. He threw the ha'penny Mr Coyne had given him. 'Did you enjoy yourself, Tom?' Holy Mullihan said as they walked back along the promenade.

Tom said he had. He'd never thought knife-throwing would be as good as that. He'd never forget it when the man had put the handkerchief around his eyes, when the two girls screamed. He'd never forget a minute of it, he said.

'D'you remember the word I told you, Tom?' Holy Mullihan enquired when they were back in South Main Street, where the music, which had started again, was less noisy. 'D'you remember what I was explaining to you?'

Tom nodded, in the hope that the conversation would not be repeated.

'Illegitimate is what we have to say, Tom. The way a person is born.'

Tom explained to Holy Mullihan what he had explained before: that his father and mother had been unable to get married due to the fact that his father had been killed. They would have been married the same week, he said. His father had the wedding ring bought. He had furniture bought for the gate-lodge.

'I know all that, Tom. You told me.'

Humpy Geehan called out to them, but Holy Mullihan didn't answer. 'You're not in doubt when you say your Hail Mary, Tom?' he said. 'You know every word of it?'

'I do of course.'

'Don't be sure of yourself, Tom. We're not put on earth to be sure of ourselves.'

Tom didn't understand that. He began to ask, but changed his mind. 'I have to turn off here,' he said when they came to Narrow Lane. 'I have to go down the quays.'

Holy Mullihan continued on his way with him. There were other words that the boys at the Christian Brothers' might use, he said, but they'd all mean the same thing. Having the ring bought didn't make any difference.

'He couldn't help getting killed,' Tom said.

'There's a story told, Tom, about St Francis of Sales. St Francis of Sales was going into heaven and they asked him for his sins, so he made a last Confession. "Another thing is," he said, "I swallowed a shred of mutton on a Friday." He ate the piece of mutton due to not knowing what day of the week it was. D'you understand that, Tom?'

'I do.'

'St Francis of Sales was turned away from heaven and had to wait a day, Tom. He made an excuse after he'd finished his Confession. If he hadn't done that he'd have walked in as he stood. D'you understand, Tom?'

'I do.'

'St Francis of Sales told the story himself. There were labourers working in a field in France and St Francis of

Sales appeared to them, coming back specially to tell that story. So's that others would be helped. D'you follow the story, Tom?'

'I understand it all right.'

'I'm glad you do, Tom.'

They had arrived at the quays, but Haverty was not there. Holy Mullihan said:

'I have other stories I'll tell you, Tom.'

Before he could do so Haverty appeared. He made his way unsteadily along the quayside, the remains of a cigarette in the middle of his mouth. It was almost dark: on the other side of the calm expanse of water you could see lights in Carriglas.

'I'll be going so,' Holy Mullihan said.

He went immediately, slipping into the gloom before Haverty was near enough to notice him. 'Is that Tom?' Haverty called out, and Tom said it was. He'd never seen anything like the knife-throwing, he added. The man had done it with his eyes bandaged. She'd stood as still as a statue.

'Did you see the ferryman, Tom? Was he here at all?'

Tom said he hadn't been. He'd only just arrived, he said.

'The old fellow has the boat tied up. Isn't that ridiculous, Tom, when he knows we're abroad? I'll have to rouse him from his bed.'

Tom waited again, listening to the music and imagining the knives cutting through the air and the woman smiling. A man in the audience had been saying that if a knife went into her head or penetrated her heart, she'd be as dead as a doornail while you'd wink.

'The young lad delayed me,' he heard Haverty saying after he'd knocked on the door of the quayside house. Tom hadn't known the ferryman lived there, and he tried to ascertain which house it was so that he could examine it in the daylight. 'Would we have a quick one before we start?' Haverty offered, and Tom heard a mumble of protest, and further cajoling from Haverty, and then the two men set off in the direction of a public house. He had to wait a while longer before they appeared again. He had never been in the ferryboat in the dark before.

'Don't mention Spillane's,' Haverty said when the water had been crossed and they were walking away from the pier. The music had accompanied them all the way across, the same couple of songs. Then suddenly, finally, it had ceased. 'Say yourself and myself went to the knife-throwing,' Haverty directed. 'Never mind about the other.' Miss Rolleston had asked him to enquire of Mr O'Hagan if he'd take charge of one of the traps or the governess-car on her wedding day, because there'd be people staying at the house who'd want conveying to the ferry. Years ago, before he passed the post office examination, Mr O'Hagan had been in charge of the stables at a house that got burnt down, and in those days he used to help at Carriglas on a social occasion. 'That's why I had to go into Spillane's,' Haverty explained. 'To ask him if he could fix to be on his holidays on August the twenty-sixth. Well, I asked him and he said he would.'

In the gate-lodge kitchen Tom's mother was darning a vest, with the lamp drawn close to where she sat. He could tell at once that she was cross, even though she didn't say anything. He could tell she was thinking she wouldn't have let him go if she'd known he'd be out so late.

'You should have come!' he exclaimed, unable to disperse his excitement. 'You never saw the like of it.'

But when she spoke it was to tell him to go in to bed. 'Hurry and wash yourself now.'

He washed at the sink. All the time he wanted to tell her about Mr Coyne and Mr O'Hagan, how he'd had biscuits and two bottles of lemonade, how Mr Coyne had given him a ha'penny to throw down for the Zodiacs. He even wanted to tell her the story Holy Mullihan had passed on to him, how St Francis of Sales had appeared in a field.

'Goodnight so,' he said.

'I'll come in in a minute.'

He took the lamp she'd lit for him while he'd been washing himself, and in the bedroom he shared with her he took his clothes off and got into bed. Before she came to bed herself she would fold across the shutters to keep the draught out. When it rained the water oozed in at the window and dripped off the windowsill, whether the shutters were drawn or not. She said it was unhealthy.

He said his prayers as he lay there, although he knew he should have knelt by the bed the way she liked him to, the way she did herself. Then he thought again about the knives flashing through the air and the woman's naked legs and arms, and the things the man had said. When he'd been standing on the quays with Holy Mullihan he'd heard other girls screaming and he'd guessed that the man was putting the scarf over his eyes.

'Goodnight so, Tom.'

She asked him if he'd said his prayers and then she took the glass off the lamp and blew the flame out. Her own lamp cast her shadow on to the wall, making her much bigger than she was.

'I'm glad you enjoyed it, Tom.'

When she kissed him he knew her crossness had gone. His cheek retained the soft impression of her lips and he could feel her saying to him that it wasn't he who had caused the crossness, although in fact she didn't say anything. He knew it wasn't even Haverty who had caused it, by making them late. When he'd asked her once she'd said the crossness came and went, caused by nothing at all.

3. Cornelius Dowley

Honeysuckle again scented the dusty road, the fuchsia hedges reddened. Villana and her grandmother had tea beneath the strawberry trees, Tom went on his usual errands. By July the iron supports of the bridge had been set in concrete, twelve on the mainland, twelve on the island. Alien, perfectly upright, the line of their height on either side sloping to meet the level of the land, their graceless presence was only ugly. The girders that were to stretch between them lay among rocks and gorse, those resting on the ground lost in a growth of cowparsley and meadow daisies. Sheds of corrugated iron had been erected, trees felled, undergrowth cleared. The place of the bridge had already acquired a personality that had not been there before, a fleeting spirit of its own, imposed by labourers.

In the Rose of Tralee boarding-house, on a hot afternoon of that same July, Mrs Moledy ran the tip of her tongue over her lips and called John James her king. Earlier she had sprinkled the sheets with eau de Cologne, which was her way. As casually as she could manage, she said:

'Darling, is there no chance at all I could be invited?'

'Invited to what?'

'The wedding breakfast, pet. I wouldn't come to the church; that wouldn't be permitted for me. But what harm would there be in attending the breakfast afterwards? I'd only stay five minutes.'

He made a motion with his head, indicative of shaking it.

He'd had to walk through litter because the summer visitors had arrived. It was a disgrace, the litter there was in the streets, cigarette-packets and sweet-papers everywhere, orange peel and banana skins. The promenade was a holy show, no better than a zoo.

'I would love above everything to be invited, darling.'

He couldn't arrange it, he protested. There was nothing he could do. After a silence, Mrs Moledy said:

'Is there a chance we could have the wedding breakfast in the Rose of Tralee, darling?'

'*Here*? Here, in this house?'

'Why not, pet?'

'People would think it strange.'

Mrs Moledy did not accept that. She'd had a world of experience in catering, she pointed out. She cooked food for her boarders every day of her life; when the house was full she was run off her feet and still she managed. It wouldn't be the first wedding breakfast there had been at the Rose of Tralee; a day-and-night licence was easily obtained, midnight to midnight, any alcoholic beverage you'd care to name.

'Absolutely impossible.'

She pouted. In a moment she said:

'Darling, I'd do anything to be pals with Villana.'

'Pals?'

'To be able to say hullo to her. To get on to terms, pet.'

'Say hullo to her in a shop. She goes into Lett's and the London and Newcastle.'

'It'll be unusual for poor Villana, what she has to face now.'

He did not understand this, so said nothing. His sister was marrying the man; she had chosen to and she intended to. You couldn't control Villana.

'There's things your sister should know. There's things I could say to her.'

She went on talking and he occupied himself by trying to remember the name of the carpentry instructor at school. He could see him quite clearly, a small, bald-headed man with a foul pipe. He'd had a nickname, but that was difficult to recall also.

'Going into Balt's bed,' she was saying. 'And she unused to that side of things.'

The man had worn a brown coat in the carpentry shop, presumably to keep the sawdust off him. He used to light his pipe from a gas jet he always kept going, under the glue-pot.

'There'll be a lot of talk, darling, on account the wedding breakfast isn't being held in the Rose of Tralee.'

My God, would she never cease? Of course there wouldn't be talk. There wasn't a soul besides herself who imagined it a natural thing that the wedding party should be held in a seedy seafront boarding-house instead of at Carriglas.

'It's how it was in the past,' he patiently explained. 'Always at the house.'

'Darling, you go on too much about the past. The future is what you and me have to think about. Sure, you're only a boy.'

'I'm thirty-five.'

'You were too young ever to have gone to that war, pet. You'd still be a soldier if you'd stayed at home.'

The conversation was pointless. If he hadn't a damaged leg he'd still be in the army: it was ridiculous to go on repeating the fact, the way she apparently liked to.

'I often think of you in your uniform,' she said.

He did not comment, instead made a fresh effort to remember the carpentry instructor's name. The man had been showing Asquith-Jones how to cut a dovetail one day and suddenly he'd lost his temper because Asquith-Jones hadn't been paying proper attention. He'd struck poor old Asquith with the flat side of a panel saw.

'He could easily be her father,' she was saying. 'If he's a day he could be her father.'

'Are you talking about my sister's fiancé?'

'He's a right peculiarity, you know.'

He saw no reason to agree, even though he shared the opinion. He said instead that the solicitor was as God had seen fit to make him. Comment was impolite, he sought to imply with his tone.

'All I'm saying to you, darling, is there's not so many years between ourselves.'

'What d'you mean?'

'What age would you say I was, Jack?'

He turned his head away, wincing because of all her modes of addressing him he disliked most her uninvited use of his father's name. He had never wondered about her age. She was a widow was all he had ever thought, the daughter of a publican in Cahir, she'd once let drop. Her husband had died of a burst appendix, she'd let drop also.

'I'm thirty-nine years old, Jack. Four years the difference.'

'You look older than thirty-nine.'

She pouted, protruding her lower lip. Beneath the sheet she drew away from him.

'I'm no good at guessing ages.' He had spoken casually, simply stating the truth. He endeavoured to make amends because he knew that was necessary. 'I always think people are older than they are.'

'I'd marry you tomorrow, Jack.'

Unfortunately, he was unable to prevent himself from giving a laugh, even though he was well aware it would cause trouble. A display of amusement was the last thing that went down well; he had experience of that. When less outrageous suggestions had been made he'd been unable to prevent himself from giving a laugh, too.

'You treat me like I'm a strumpet.'

'Ah no, no.' Again he sought to make amends, but he

knew it was too late. The day she'd addressed him on the promenade he'd hardly been able to believe it, especially when she'd asked him if he'd like to come into the Rose of Tralee boarding-house. She enjoyed showing people around it, she said, and all the time she was talking he could smell the perfume she was wearing and he couldn't help staring straight at her bosom, cocked out at him and quivering. Her large mouth shone with lipstick. She'd patted her hair in a way he found exciting.

'You have no respect for me. You take what you can get.'

He denied that in a consolatory voice. She often misunderstood things, he protested. He enjoyed her company.

'Errah, don't tell me lies. D'you think I'm brainless? D'you think I'm some type of a jellyfish you have relations with? And what d'you consider you are yourself, boy? Did you ever do a hand's turn in your life?'

He rose immediately. Standing naked, he quietly said he would not be spoken to like that. Unexpectedly, and for a most unpleasant moment, he imagined his father looking down at him from beyond the dead, and then looking away in extreme distaste. This was definitely the end, he stated in the same quiet tone; a conclusion had been reached in the relationship.

'Ridiculous tantrums,' she said.

He moved away and drew his clothes on, keeping to one side of the net curtains in case he should be glimpsed from the street. It was nonsense that she was only thirty-nine, more like fifty. Had she gone insane that she could mention marriage, that she could contemplate being the mistress of Carriglas?

'The man selling fish was talking about you the other day,' she casually remarked, and when he displayed no interest she repeated the information.

'What the fishmonger says is his own business.'

'Isn't it interesting, though, he would have the cheek?'

He knotted his tie and bent to attend to his shoelaces. He

had no wish to remain in the room, hearing a fishmonger's conversation at second hand. He said so, not raising his voice.

'I will tell you this,' she said, 'which I heard from that same man. The bridge will be called after Cornelius Dowley.'

He looked up, the end of a lace between his fingers. 'Is that true?' he said after a moment.

'What d'you mean true, darling?'

'Is it like the Confession thing?'

'What Confession thing?'

'You pretended a certain state of affairs in order to annoy me.'

'Come back into the bed, honey.'

'Is it true about the bridge?'

'I'm only repeating what I was told by the fish man. Sure, does it matter, Jack? Didn't Dowley get the works from the Tans? Dowley's dust and old bones by now, honey.'

He completed the tying of his shoelaces, then straightened up. He buttoned his waistcoat and drew on his jacket.

'Is it true?' he said again.

'I never told you a lie, boy.'

That in itself was a lie, but he knew by looking at her that what she was reporting about the bridge was the truth. More than once it had crossed John James's mind that the bridge might be given a title of some kind; he had even imagined permission being sought for his father's name to be carved on a stone. The Rollestons were the island family; they had been humane at the time of the potato blight; they had given generously, seeking no reward. Words on the bridge might have remembered that, through a memorial to one of them.

'Ah, pet, don't go being a crosspatch. Didn't I tell you I'd lend you the money for a motor-car? I wouldn't go back on a promise, pet, no matter what you say to me.'

'We don't need a motor-car.'

'Come back into bed, honey.'

She made a kissing sound, smiling at him. She threw the bedclothes back and held her breasts towards him. She told him to forget about the bridge, she told him to forget about everything. There was no one like him, she said. 'Don't be a crosspatch,' she urged again.

'I'm not a crosspatch.'

He longed to do as she invited. He longed to loosen his tie and slip it from his neck. He longed to undo the buttons of his waistcoat with dawdling anticipation, and to be drawn again into the warmth of her bulk. But he shook his head and left the bedroom.

*

'There's a thing I have to tell you, Tom,' his mother said in the kitchen of the gate-lodge. She turned from the range and placed his tea in front of him: a plate of fried bread and a narrow rasher of bacon. 'The bridge is going to be called after Cornelius Dowley.'

Tom knew. They'd been talking about it in the convent. 'Shh,' one of the girls had reprimanded, suddenly realising that among all the renowned exploits of Cornelius Dowley there was the blowing to pieces of Tom's father in mistake for someone else.

'I heard it,' he said.

'What did they say, Tom?'

'Only that.'

He cut the bacon and a piece of fried bread to go with it. He returned his knife and fork to the plate between each mouthful, the way she liked him to. 'Hey, look,' a boy called Slattery had said once, pointing at the steps of the old billiard-hall. 'That's where the Tans shot Corny Dowley.' A padlock secured the doors of the billiard-hall now, but if you climbed up to one of the windows you could see the three billiard tables inside, with big square-shaded lights hanging close above their green surfaces. There were cigarette-butts on the floor and a broken glass in a corner. 'Corny Dowley was a great fellow,' Slattery had said.

Beside him at the table, his mother poured what remained of the fat from the frying-pan into a bowl, adding it to dripping that had already set. She ran water on to the pan at the sink and put it to steep on the draining-board. She returned to the range, saying she'd black-lead the parts of it that weren't hot.

'It's unfortunate they decided that,' she said.

When the girl had mentioned about the bridge, and when the girls she was with had looked in his direction, he'd felt shy but he hadn't been upset. He hadn't been upset at the billiard-hall when Slattery had said Corny Dowley was a great fellow, although he'd already known that Corny Dowley had been responsible for his father's death. He'd never even seen a photograph of his father.

'Dowley came from the island,' his mother said. 'That's why they're doing it.'

'I heard he came from here.'

Corny Dowley's best-remembered exploit was the ambush at Lahane crossroads. Brother Meagher from the Christian Brothers' had arrived at the convent specially one morning, to take the class to see the place – a mile out of the town on the back road behind the slaughterhouse. But long before that Tom had heard the story of a man lying waiting for half a night in a ditch at Lahane crossroads. Four other men had been crouched behind the stone walls that skirted the roads which met there; all of them had their fingers on the triggers of their rifles. Less than a quarter of a mile away the road from Mallow was mined to catch the Black and Tans, and when the first lorry was blown up the soldiers in the lorries behind it made their way forward on foot and walked into the trap at the crossroads. In the end nineteen Black and Tans lay dead, scattered around the blown-up lorry and at the crossroads, and there was more to the story still. While the remaining forces in the neighbourhood were searching for those responsible, Cornelius Dowley and his companions raided the barracks and carried away a haul of guns and ammunition. Nothing more daring had been perpetrated in the neighbourhood, or carried out so skilfully.

At Lahane crossroads, while Brother Meagher retailed all that again, Tom had imagined the man from the island lying in one of the deeply dug ditches, and the tips of the rifles poking out through the stones of the walls. He imagined the great explosion there had been, the waiting men not moving when they heard it, intent on watching for the remaining Black and Tans to appear out of the dust and the smoke. 'Like devils they came,' Brother Meagher said.

Brother Meagher's eyebrows met across his forehead. There was something the matter with his fingernails which prevented them from growing. He had dark jowls, and opaque eyes that became excited when he talked about the heroes and martyrs of the past: this was his particular subject. Addressing the class at the crossroads, he related how – generations before the time of Corny Dowley – the head of an obstreperous tenant-farmer had been stuck on to the sharpened branch of a tree on this very spot, a warning that obedience was expected. Corny Dowley would have known it, he said, and would maybe have smiled over the shadow the tree still cast as he waited in the ditch. 'D'you see the shadow now?' Brother Meagher continued, pointing through the sunlight at the dark outline on the road. The shadow was special, he said.

While he ate his bacon and fried bread and while his mother began the black-leading of the range, Tom reminded her of that excursion to Lahane crossroads. 'Time enough for Meagher to be getting at you,' she'd said at the time. Neck Daly and Deso Furphy, who'd left the convent last summer to go on to the Christian Brothers', said that

Brother Meagher chalked up the names of heroes and martyrs on the blackboard and you had to learn them off. You had to remember that the life of a martyr was cut short because he wouldn't salute a heresy, or bend to a foreign foe. If you didn't know that off pat you'd get the strap. You had to remember when Brother Meagher touched the name *Daniel O'Connell* with the tip of his cane that Daniel O'Connell was the Liberator. Neck Daly said once that Daniel O'Connell had died in his bed after drinking too much Italian whiskey. Holy Mullihan reported him and he got the strap for telling lies.

'You'll need to behave yourself with the Brothers, Tom,' his mother said when he reminded her of all that now. 'It's not like with the nuns.'

'Ah sure, I know it isn't.'

He was nervous about going on to the Brothers, but one good thing was that by the time he got there Holy Mullihan would have left. They usually went away altogether when they were going to become priests; Holy Mullihan mightn't even be about the streets any more. Cathal Lenihan, who was the same age as Tom, couldn't make up his mind whether he was called for the priesthood or the Brothers. 'Well, what are ye all going to be?' Father Pierce had asked one day when he came in to hear the catechism, and Cathal Lenihan had explained his dilemma. 'The Christian Brothers are a fine body of men,' Father Pierce had said, and added jokingly: 'We won't comment on the priests.' Two girls had put up their hands when he asked if there was any girl present who was aiming to be a nun, and he said that was great. Then Derek Birthistle said he was going into Burke's the auctioneers like his father, and Cluck Walsh that he was all set for America. 'There's a lot of us in America,' Father Pierce commented. 'You won't lack for companions, Cluck.' He mentioned the man who had given the town the piece of land for recreation purposes after he'd become a candy king in San Francisco. There was many a story of a poor Irish boy ending up in some city like San Francisco, or New York or Chicago. 'Don't forget us in that case,' he said to Cluck Walsh, and everyone laughed because they knew Cluck Walsh wouldn't get more than a yard out of the town.

'There's people might mention it to you,' Tom's mother said, not turning round from the range, 'about the bridge. And maybe about how your father and myself were a week off getting married. Take no notice of that talk, Tom.'

He might have told her about Holy Mullihan when she said that. He might have told her that sometimes the girls on the ferryboat looked at him interestedly, that Sister Sullivan always looked at him as if he'd done something wrong, that he felt Brother Meagher didn't like him. Father Pierce had once stopped specially when he saw him, on the street outside Barry's. 'You've more prayers to say than others, Tom,' was what the priest had said. 'But I wouldn't agree that was a bad thing. Never object to getting down on your knees, Tom.'

'I'll take no notice,' he promised his mother, not knowing why he pretended no one had ever said anything at all. He'd never even mentioned Holy Mullihan to her.

'You're not forgetting to keep the well tidy?' she said, returning the black-lead and the brushes to the cupboard she'd taken them from. She had a smudge of the black-lead on her forehead, and he drew her attention to it because she'd be cross if she went to the house like that, the way she was when she'd gone up with a mark of egg yolk on her overall.

'I'll go over to the well tomorrow.'

'It's great you look after it, Tom.'

She left the kitchen soon afterwards to go up and cook the Rollestons' dinner for them, and as soon as she'd gone he remembered he should have asked her to bring him back a piece of butter-paper to trace a map on. The bays and harbours had to be marked in and named. Next week it would be the mountains, the week after it would be the rivers. 'Ask your mother for a bit of butter-paper,' Sister Sullivan always advised when a map had to be traced, and if anyone raised a hand to say there wouldn't be butter-paper in the house she would reply that in that case it would have to be obtained elsewhere. 'No good attending school if you don't assist yourselves,' Sister Sullivan often said. 'You might as well stop back in the fields.'

So Tom ran after his mother and asked her on the avenue if she'd bring him back a piece of butter-paper. She said she would. She said she'd leave it on the kitchen table and he could draw the map in the morning, before he went to school.

'It was here it happened,' she said, pointing at a spot a few yards away. 'It was here your father was killed.'

There was nothing different about that part of the avenue. The moss on the surface was the same shade of green as it was elsewhere. The rhododendrons on either side looked as though they had never been disturbed by an explosion.

'I didn't know it was here.'

His mother was still staring at the place, and he realised now that she was upset because the bridge was to be called after Corny Dowley. You could tell it by the way she touched her cheeks with the tops of her fingers, and walked away without saying anything else.

*

In the outhouse that was his workshop a paraffin lamp burned steadily on the old mahogany dressing-table Lionel remembered in his father's room when he was a child. He and Haverty had carried it out of the back scullery a year ago so that he might repair one of its legs, but he had not yet done so. He wasn't sure that he could; in the end he would probably abandon it.

He picked up the lamp and shone it about him before he

left the outhouse. Seed-boxes were stacked in a corner. A new cross-shaft for a gate was still clamped in the vice, where he'd been planing it. The potato sacks which Mrs Haverty had recently patched hung from a hook, tied together in a bundle.

He closed the outhouse door and crossed the yard with the lamp still alight, his sheepdogs close behind him. He said goodnight to them and watched them disappear in the gloom before he passed into the scullery corridor. 'You'll have heard about the bridge?' Haverty had said as they walked back from the fields that evening. 'They're going to remember Dowley with it.'

At dinner that news had been present at the table, though mentioned by no one. Villana had spoken of something the dressmaker had passed on when she'd visited the house that morning, to do with a nephew's promotion in the Guards. John James, as always on a Monday evening, had not said much. 'Have you the hay in cocks?' his grandmother had asked him, and Lionel had replied that the hay was safe.

In the silent, empty kitchen he made tea, pouring boiling water from the kettle that had been left for him on the range, and rooting in a tin box for the biscuits he liked. He had been in the town on the day of Dowley's funeral. He had watched the cheap cortège going slowly to the church, the blinds of shops and houses drawn, men pulling off their caps and blessing themselves. That morning Cornelius Dowley's mother had drowned herself, as if she'd been unable to bear the ordeal of this occasion. He'd thought of that as he stood there, and then had been overcome by a strange confusion. He had wanted to walk at the end of the procession.

He broke another biscuit in half and ate it slowly.

*

Carriglas, July 14th, 1931. I dreamed last night of an afternoon one summer when Hugh was here. They were not children any more, and I had become their companion rather than being in charge of them. We walked, all of us, to the tennis-court among the trees, and later the maids brought lemonade and stood to watch. 'How greatly Sarah has improved!' Lionel said. I was first aware then that Villana and my brother were in love.

Nothing was different in my dream from the afternoon itself. John James was carefree and had the manner of his father, and in my dream I was reminded how I had imagined him one day the master of Carriglas, and had imagined the household as it would be, another family growing up.

'Do you remember,' I asked Lionel tonight, 'that afternoon years ago when you complimented me on my tennis?' I reminded him of the maids bringing the lemonade and then remaining. He smiled obligingly, but clearly he has no memory for such occasions. I was in love myself that afternoon.

'Lett's have sent over these summer shirts,' he said tonight, spreading them out on the kitchen table. He would take the first one, not even unfolding the others. I laughed at him and he laughed too. Together we choose two, both of them green, the colour that suits him best.

*

Mrs Rolleston sat in the armchair by her window, looking out over the sea at the dwindling lights of the town. On the dressing-table at the far end of the room a lamp burned beside an oval looking-glass, its light gleaming on her scent bottles and on the ivory backs of her hairbrushes.

I heard about the bridge, the letter she'd just opened informed her. Quite often she didn't open the letters immediately, but put them aside until she'd gathered strength. *That's great for Corny but there is only sympathy in my heart for yourselves, the way things are. I wouldn't ask you for it at a time like this but fifteen shillings in an envelope would be an act of charity. Only I had bad luck a week ago.*

When the Black and Tans shot Dowley on the billiard-hall steps Kathleen Quigley had wept as inconsolably as Brigid had less than a month earlier. It would have been unthinkable to allow them to go on working side by side in the same kitchen, and in Brigid's condition it would have been a cruelty to turn her out. 'D'you understand?' she said, but Kathleen Quigley had crossly shaken her head.

Mrs Rolleston rose and prepared herself for bed. As she washed she wondered if the woman managed to live on the money sent her. The letters sometimes mentioned the hens she kept, and they had also mentioned the death of her father and, some years later, of her mother. The Havertys had insisted at the time that Dowley would never have looked at a girl like Kathleen Quigley, that it was only her hopes that had been destroyed, not any kind of reality. *There was never hard feelings on my side*, all the letters ended. *And never will be.*

The maid's elongated face came into Mrs Rolleston's mind, and her thin nose and her long front teeth. Trying not to see it, she brushed her hair in front of the looking-glass, gazing instead at her own reflection. 'There's a telegram after coming, ma'am': it was that same maid who had held it towards her, standing in the drawing-room in her after-noon black. She hadn't opened it until the girl had gone, until she'd heard her footsteps passing through the hall. 'This isn't true,' she'd whispered before she read the message, knowing what the message contained. In the drawing-room she had sat with the piece of paper between her fingers, and then had torn it in half and then into quarters and then into tiny scraps. A chaffinch had flown through the open French windows and she had watched it flying about the room.

She carried the lamp to the table beside her bed and turned the wick down. When Villana had come into the drawing-room the bird was perched on a picture. She had told Villana immediately that her father was no longer alive, and later Lionel had come to where she sat on the sofa, with the torn-up telegram still in her lap. The news had been sent by the regiment, she explained to them. John James, probably not far from where the death had occurred, would have been informed by the regiment also: when there was a war you had always to be prepared for news from the regiment. She had gone with his children to the study where every day he had read the *Irish Times*, where his things were as he'd left them – the shotgun on the wall, the fishing-rods in the corner, the bric-à-brac on the ochre-coloured table cover. 'I don't know what we'll do,' she said, unable to think of anything else to say.

The sheets of her bed were cold. She pulled a shawl about her shoulders. Was it because of all that, her only child taken from her, that she had shared so acutely Brigid's distress years later, and Kathleen Quigley's distress also? She sighed, not answering her question, only knowing that three men had died unnecessarily, all of them connected with Carriglas. Best not to dwell too long on it; these were not thoughts for night-time. The Camiers of Unionhall had been invited to the wedding, and Lady Rossboyne and the Bishop of Killaloe. She'd been a Camier herself, though not of Unionhall. Tattie Rossboyne had been a Camier too; the woman who'd married the clergyman an Ennis. Villiers Hadnett had been invited from Athlone, her side of the family also. All these people would have to stay in the house. Heaven alone knew why Villana was bothering with Villiers Hadnett, or the Camiers of Unionhall if it came to that. No Rolleston was coming because none was left. Sarah and Hugh were the only connected Pollexfens, apart from Hugh's children. Naturally Hugh wouldn't come.

She dozed, and then fell into a deeper sleep. She dreamed that Villana came into the room to play with the scent bottles on the dressing-table, lifting from them their glass stoppers, her sharply blue eyes lost in concentration when, one by one, she smelt the perfumes. Then Villana was dusting ornaments in Finnamore Balt's house and the ash from her cigarette kept falling on to them and Villana kept laughing, saying it didn't matter. 'This poor dear man,' she said. 'I'm ruining his peace of mind.'

A child ran across the island, but it was not one of her grandchildren, nor her son, and it was not Tom. The child had red hair. He ran over the rocks and the heather and the gorse. He clambered down a cliffside and ran on the shingle of the shore and then on the sand. 'What's his name?' Finnamore Balt said, serving the food in the dining-room, holding out a dish of carrots to her. The red-haired boy hid himself in a cave, but then he had to run on again. He had to climb up the cliff at Elador's Bay because there was nowhere else to go. 'That boy was killed at Passchendaele,' Finnamore Balt said, but she contradicted that, reminding him that it was Villana's father who had been killed at Passchendaele. 'Then he was killed on your avenue,' Finnamore Balt said, but she knew that was wrong also. 'Mr Balt asked me to marry him,' Brigid said, looking up from the bread she was making, her face delighted in the kitchen. And Linchy came in and said the man who'd taken his life from him had had his name put on a metal plaque. *He died for our fair land*, the pronouncement declared, and Kathleen Quigley said it was a holy disgrace, that Brigid was staying on and she was being asked to leave.

Abruptly, Mrs Rolleston awoke, her dream still vivid. Recently, Finnamore Balt had begun to haunt her dreams, appearing in all sorts of rôles, like a figure in a fantastic comedy. It would be after midnight by now. The last twinkle of lights on the sea would be extinguished, and darkness would be there until dawn. She imagined the silent town, and walking from the quays to church, of going into Meath's, which she used to quite often, of walking up to the bandstand.

Again she closed her eyes, hoping that sleep would come, but it didn't immediately. The red-haired boy ran over the rocks again, his feet bare, the jersey he wore ragged. He ran on the paths the sheep made in the heather, and by the edge of the sea because the sand was easier to run on than the shingle was. 'He is myself when young,' Finnamore Balt said in another dream, and everyone in the dining-room laughed.

4. Wedding Preparations

'It's like you'd walk up to the Cross and spit on Our Lord,' Holy Mullihan said. 'When your mother committed the sin, Tom, another thorn was established in the crown.'

A sin of that type, Holy Mullihan added, would afflict the child who came out of it. The sin would only go from a person after death, and then only if there'd been penance enough and sufficient Hail Marys said. 'There would be people who'd be frightened of the sin, Tom. They wouldn't mean harm to an afflicted person, only it's the way they'd see it. You might see them crossing a street if they saw you coming. Another thing is, they mightn't like to touch you.'

In the town the summer crowds increased. They spread themselves on the sand, each family claiming a length of breakwater to hang their bathing towels on. They spent all day in the sunshine, were cooled by the seaside breeze, and returned at half-past five to the boarding-houses of the promenade. Bookmakers and publicans, insurance sales-men, commercial travellers: all came with their families and stayed a week. St Vincent de Paul excursions brought trains full of slum children for a day by the sea.

When they tired of the strand the visitors climbed the sandhills beyond the promenade, where an old woman kept a shop during the summer months. This was a small black hut of corrugated iron standing by itself and selling what-ever the old woman wheeled in her pram to it each day, usually an assortment of Willwood's sweets and the rock-cakes she sold at two a penny. She was accompanied by a small dog with a yapping bark that most of the time frightened the visitors away. Sometimes a lone man would walk among the pampas grass of the hills, with a newspaper like a baton under his arm. Sometimes a couple would wander in search of seclusion.

The people of the town varied in their reception of the visitors and were affected differently by the summer weather that attracted them. The poor remained in their lanes and cottages, their half-doors closed, their babies impatient for food. On Sundays the poor brought the smell of poverty to Mass, but they did not ever choose to venture on to the promenade, nor to mingle with the visitors.

Those more fortunately placed had no such inhibitions. Mrs Coyne, the garage proprietor's wife, gathered her eleven girls around her and took them to play on the sands. Sister Teresa Dolores and Sister Sullivan moved discreetly through the sunshine, their beads and crucifixes dangling, their habits rustling. Mr O'Hagan from the post office was seen on the seafront every Sunday evening; Finnamore Balt walked the length of the promenade every day. Guard Ryan and Willie Troy from Meath's raced their bicycles on the damp sand in the early morning, and at that time of day also three priests went swimming. Father Pierce called out warnings about jellyfish or the lowness of the sea's temperature, but his companions kept their voices quiet. They were older, pale-skinned men, the smaller of them with a head shaped like a bullet, a resemblance that was more noticeable when he was denuded of his black clothes. The head of the other was a tiny knob at the top of his white body and was more noticeable then also, like the head of a pin.

The Pierrots came to perform on the sands. Duffy's Circus came and went, and then Toft's Roundabouts and Bumper Cars attracted the visitors to the wasteland that might one day become the Father Ignatius Quirke Park. In Traynor's Picture Palace tales of romance and gangsters and the Wild

West unfolded nightly. In the Protestant church of St Boniface Canon Kinchella preached sermons that had become familiar to his congregation. In the Church of Our Lady the summer feast days were celebrated. 'Take a gander at that, sir,' invited Mr Coyne, drawing John James by the sleeve of his jacket into his garage. He pointed at a large vehicle with its roof folded down. Of French manufacture, he declared, owned in the past by a titled person. But John James replied that he had no money.

Eugene Prille, the solicitor's clerk, found homes for both the solicitor's maid and his white cat. Harbinson, the solicitor's partner, agreed to be his best man. The dressmaker, Miss Laffey, completed the wedding dress that Villana had ordained should be simple. 'I often see you alone,' Brother Meagher accused Tom in South Main Street. 'I see you about, you're never out with a gang. Mahoney and John Joe Reilly are boys of your own age. Why aren't you out with them?'

He peered at Tom from beneath the eyebrows that met across his forehead, and Tom said to himself that Brother Meagher was already waiting for him behind the green railings of the Christian Brothers'. Already he was looking forward to the day when he could knock the badness out of him.

'I don't belong to a gang,' Tom said.

'I'm saying that to you, boy.'

'I go about alone.'

'I'm saying that to you too. Are you stupid, boy?'

Tom didn't know if he was stupid or not. He didn't mind not belonging to a gang. Holy Mullihan didn't belong to a gang and no one thought the worse of him for that. Neck Daly and Deso Furphy went around together, but just the two of them could hardly be called a gang.

'I'll be looking for improvement in you,' Brother Meagher warned.

In Spillane's public house further racing tips were

deplored; Butt Nolan was abused in his absence. In Myley Flynn's, Briscoe, the porter at the Provincial Bank, heard how a woman, swimming on her own one midday, had swum into difficulties and been rescued. She'd lain unconscious for twenty minutes on the sand, her face gone blue, but in the end recovered. Afterwards, hurrying about his business on the streets, Briscoe told of this, exaggerating the drama only slightly.

Few of the summer visitors took the ferry to the island in order to wander along the cliffs, or to view the abbey ruins or climb up to the standing stones. But some women of the town, at the end of the first week in August, made their annual pilgrimage to the holy well. The saint whose hermit habitation the place had been, whose life there had inspired the lives of the abbey monks, was venerated on a day associated with his memory. The stone reputed to have been his pillow was touched by the women; rosaries were told above the moist clay.

Villana, wearing a plain yellow dress, passed through the gates of Carriglas on the afternoon following the day of the summer's pilgrimage. She turned from the road to follow the stream that ran down to the abbey, where sheep nibbled the grass between the stones that had fallen from the walls. Here and there remained the shape of a gothic window. Steps led halfway up a tower, dwindling to nothing, as the tower itself did. There was a cell of discernible proportions. Once upon a time plots had been tilled in a surrounding garden, bees kept, fish brought from the river and the sea. The monks had sheltered quietly, fearful of invasion, while the lords of the mainland boisterously argued at a distance. But the shattering of that tranquillity had come; the monks had disappeared, the walls had fallen down.

On her unchanging walk Villana passed through the abbey, and by the holy well. She climbed through woodland to emerge at the foot of a grassy hillock, and then climbed on, to its summit and the ring of slender stones on the burial ground that pre-dated by centuries the achievement of the monks. From here she could see the sea again, the grey shadow of Carriglas, and in the greater distance the clutter of the town. After she had stood for a moment she picked some sea-pinks. They grew differently on the island, deeper in colour than she had ever seen them elsewhere, and seeming to go well with the black rock of its promontories and the stunted little oaks of its windswept cliffs. On maps she had seen that the island was shaped like a snail, curling in the grey-green water, at its heart this grave where kings were laid. She sat on the grass with her back against one of the standing stones, and felt in the pocket of her dress for her cigarettes and lighter. Smoking, she gave herself up to the warmth of the sun on her skin and the shimmer of the distant water. The sky was cloudless; there was no wind.

The nursery-schoolroom was to become her married bedroom. The butterflies had been swept up from the floor, the windows thrown open, the curtains taken down and washed. Her regiment of dolls remained because Finnamore had protested that it was a shame to see them go, but the table where she had once sat over her lessons, close to the fire, had been taken from the room. A bed had been set up between the fireplace and the windows; wardrobe, dressing-table, wash-stand and a chest of drawers had been carried in.

Other rooms were being made ready for the guests who would stay at Carriglas for the wedding. It was ages since so many visitors' rooms had been prepared. Once upon a time, before her own time, the Viceroy had spent ten days of August at Carriglas, a tradition that had passed from one Viceroy to the next. Less eminent visitors had stayed for months.

No word had come from Hugh. She'd thought it might, a line or two of good wishes, some sort of sign. Might he be angry? she had wondered. 'I don't want to live without you, Villana': she heard his voice, as girls heard the echo of their lovers' voices in the novels she borrowed from the convent library. In the novels she loved it when whatever was wrong became right – when the amnesia of a soldier's shell-shock lifted, when a tyrannical father relented, or a mother gave up her son to his bride with a contented heart. Happening as tenderly as any of that, Hugh might yet confess that his marriage to some girl in Essex was all made up; and looking into one another's faces, they might say they had been fools. What on earth did it matter? they might say: why shouldn't they snatch at happiness? She closed her eyes and saw him on the avenue with his leather suitcase, returning to Carriglas.

Villana finished her cigarette before she continued her walk, steeply downhill to the pier, which the ferryboat had just reached. Having turned off its engines, the ferryman was sitting on a fish crate, smoking a cigarette himself.

'I wanted to invite you,' Villana said as she approached him, 'to come up to the house on the twenty-sixth. You know what day that is?'

'I do of course, miss. It's good you'd invite an old fellow.'

'We're sorry the ferry is coming to an end.'

'You'll be better off with the bridge in the long way.'

'We're used to the ferry.'

She walked along the shore and took the path by the old boathouse to the garden, where her grandmother was sitting in the shade of the strawberry trees, a white-brimmed hat protecting her further from the afternoon sun. Villana rid her shoes of the dust they had gathered by drawing them, first one and then the other, sideways over the grass. Then she kicked them off.

'I told the ferryman to come up for a drink.'

'That's nice of you.'

'It's a natural thing to do.'

Patty arrived with a tray and a tablecloth. The cloth was spread on the table that stood among the chairs, cups and saucers arranged. Before the maid went away Villana handed her the sea-pinks and asked her to put them in water.

'I will surely, miss.'

Another wedding present had arrived: a set of Waterford decanters. Villana described them to her grandmother and, listening to the description, Mrs Rolleston nodded several times. Villana mentioned the wedding luncheon.

'Sea trout and turbot,' she said. 'Salads to go with them. Everything cold if we're to be outside.'

Again her grandmother nodded.

'And ham, I suppose, better be ordered from Meath's,' Villana stipulated. 'Not everyone cares for fish.'

'You'll have music, of course?'

'*Music?*'

'There was always music after a wedding at Carriglas. The band playing in the alcove on the stairs. Dancing all over the place.'

'Oh, I don't think that would be possible. To start with, we couldn't afford a band.'

The old woman did not acknowledge that. She sipped her tea. Then she said:

'I wish you wouldn't go on with this foolishness.'

'I've chosen this foolishness. I've actually made a choice.'

Villana picked up her book, from where she'd left it on the grass before going for her walk. '*But, my dear girl, we can all do perfectly well without happiness,*' a line of dialogue maintained. Some wise old gentleman was speaking, a traveller who had climbed the mountains of four continents and seen nature in the raw. '*The other side of the coin, my dear, is that no one can do without love. It is the greatest of all deprivations not to know love in some wise, either to give or to receive. It hardly matters which.*'

She nodded over the words, agreeing with the sentiment. But what the novel didn't say was that love left an emptiness behind that was as cold as frozen snow. The lonely cigarette in the middle of the night, the pages of another story turned, the balm of Traynor's picture house, the dream of Hugh returning to Carriglas: none of them lasted long. Only love itself, offered from whatever source, could warm, just a little, those fathomless depths: Hugh, too, knew that.

'I'll be all right, you know,' she said, as gently as she could.

But Mrs Rolleston seemed not to hear.

*

Finnamore, while tea was taken at Carriglas, held up his arms to facilitate the tailor who fitted him with his wedding suit. It seemed proper that new clothes should have been cut and made for him, even though he possessed other clothes that might have done. Villana had agreed.

'I have a bad debt, Mr Balt,' the tailor said from among the pins that lined his mouth. 'I was going to ask you to write a letter. If you would, sir.'

'Indeed I will. You mustn't put up with that.'

The tailor nodded, marking the dark cloth with his chalk. He revealed more about the nature of the debt while Finnamore courteously listened, as he always did when a misdemeanour was outlined.

'Goff,' the tailor said, naming his debtor as a member of the landowning class. 'Sir Cedric Goff owes me for four suits of plus-fours.'

'I will write Sir Cedric Goff a letter. Most certainly.'

He inclined his head as he spoke. He was pleased that this identity had been established. There were a limited number of people in the neighbourhood who would have their clothes specially made, just as there were a limited number of people who would make use of a solicitor's services, though more of course would come to Harbinson and Balt than would approach a tailor. On first hearing about the debtor, he had pondered over whom it might be; it interested him that it was Sir Cedric Goff. The initial letter would of necessity require to be delicately couched, since no doubt Sir Cedric would be present on the twenty-sixth. Eugene Prille might be given the task – in two or three lines simply to draw attention to what could be termed an oversight. When the twenty-sixth was safely past, a sterner note might be struck.

'Some constraint, is there?' the tailor enquired, buttoning the waistcoat.

Finnamore reassured him. He stood while adjustments were marked on the sleeves of the jacket, his thoughts no longer involved with Sir Cedric Goff but with four fields to which the Rollestons, beyond all possible doubt, had clear title. During all the years of his investigation he had sought a starting point, many times believing he had found it only later to become doubtful. But when recently he had suggested to the family that papers of seizure be issued he had not done so lightly. As he saw it, the Rolleston claim was indisputable; but receiving little encouragement from either his fiancée or her brothers, he had gone over the ground again, testing it for possible loopholes, probing what might be areas of weakness. He had discovered nothing to upset his sanguine view, but even so he had requested Eugene Prille to examine the ground independently. A starting point must by its very nature be indisputable; it was useless otherwise. From it, precedent would be established, and further precedent spawned.

The four fields in question were now in the hands of a woman who was only distantly connected with the family which, three generations ago, the Rollestons had excused the payment of rent. Though it was not an issue – and in Finnamore's opinion it would be unwise to suggest it ever might be – the woman in question came of fishing stock and could call on no inherited farming expertise. Deterioration of the land had set in over the years and was now continuing at a swifter pace than hitherto, the ill-drained acres separated from the Carriglas estate only by a tangle of brambles, to which the Rollestons had title also.

'Thank you, Mr Balt.' The tailor rose from a stooping position, having satisfied himself that the trouser turn-ups rested correctly on Finnamore's black shoes. 'Thank you for your patience, sir.'

Finnamore smiled an acknowledgement, his lips drawn back in bony contentment. He saw in his mind's eye the four fields joined again to the fields that had for so many centuries been their companions, a way made through the brambles, and precedent begetting precedent. He saw himself walking with his wife through gardens in which there were gardeners again, by ripening corn and healthy meadows. The prospect displeased in no particular; only the outrage of the bridge's dedication cast a shadow. He had made representations to the authorities in the sternest language at his command. Although there was no legal issue to argue, he had succinctly exposed the error of the decision that had been taken, making his case on grounds of simple humanity. *The man was the family's last enemy*, he had written in a letter that in the end covered two sheets of Harbinson and Balt writing-paper. Any day now there should be a reply.

*

Carriglas, August 10th, 1931. This afternoon I carried the can of tea to the field where Lionel and Haverty were clearing stubble. It is the first time since my return that I have done so, the task usually being Patty's, but Patty is inclined to dawdle. I went the back way, by the little copse and the hillfields, and saw the two men in the distance long before I was near enough to be noticed. I can neither describe nor properly indicate the happiness I experienced in the warm sunshine, spreading out when I arrived a tea-cloth in which I'd wrapped two slices of sponge cake. His hand brushed mine, I don't know how it was, some

accidental thing, 'Oh, sorry,' he at once apologised, rele-
gating to clumsiness on his part this precious moment.

Yet afterwards, as I walked back to the house, I felt
touched, not by contentment but by misfortune, drawn into
a mood of hopelessness that often seems to pervade the very
landscape of Carriglas now. I understand nothing of it.

*

That same evening John James walked up and down under
the monkey puzzle, smoking. He liked to do that in summer
when it was fine, as his father had. Taking his ease in the
garden after dinner, his father used to call it.

His leg ached because he was upset. 'Look on the
wash-stand, pet,' she'd said, and when he'd done so he saw
that she'd actually written out a cheque. She required no
interest on the money, she had assured him, raising herself
on an elbow and causing the bedclothes to fall back from
the upper half of her body.

His father would have laughed, even though he'd have
been surprised. People said his father was the tallest man in
Ireland and had the straightest back. His father often
permitted a whimsical slant of amusement to soften his
features; things did not upset him, but even so he could be
firm. 'Yes, I have to say surprised,' he would have drily
commented on the clandestine association.

The feeling that his father was constantly watching was
sometimes most upsetting. On his way to the boarding-
house he always hurried by the windows of the promenade
in an effort to avoid the glances by the curious; he took
exception to the haughty gaze of Finnamore Balt's white
cat, and was glad the animal was not to accompany the man
to Carriglas. All the time, striding through the summer
trippers, pushing open the door she left on the latch, he felt
uneasy. It was he who'd suggested that the maid should not
be there on Mondays; and the summer boarders were not
permitted to hang about the house during the day. 'My

handsome boy,' the woman always greeted him, no matter how they had parted the last time. And every time she did so he sensed his father's amusement.

On the lawn beneath the monkey puzzle he lit another cigarette and then continued his walk, back and forth. Somebody had spoken to Coyne about that French motor-car. Coyne wouldn't have approached him if there hadn't been a prompting. 'I didn't open my mouth to him, honey. Wouldn't it have been your sister?' But when he mentioned it at dinner Villana had appeared to be genuinely surprised. Certainly a motor-car would be necessary, his sister had agreed: her fiancé's old Ford would naturally come to Carriglas when they were married, but it was too small to accommodate the family, and besides it wasn't fair that such use should be made of it. 'In that case we'll have to sell a field,' he'd countered, separating the flesh of a sole from its backbone. Lionel had shaken his head, but hadn't said anything. A car wasn't necessary since they had several perfectly good traps, and a governess-car and a dog-cart. Besides all that, there was no call whatsoever for outside interference in a family matter; and it was typical, of course, that she'd only see it from her own point of view. 'It's only I'm worried you wouldn't make your way across to me, pet. I'm worried for yourself, getting drenched in the rain.' It was like walking into a spider's parlour, he sometimes thought. A fly with a limp might feel the way he felt, enticed into her perfume. She smiled plumply in his imagination; the bedroom statues and pictures appeared. They were the one flesh, she'd said, urging the motor-car money on him.

He sighed. The cheque had remained on the wash-stand; he'd even gone to the trouble of explaining to her that in any case a cheque was totally unacceptable because it would have to pass through the bank, her name and his on the same piece of paper. And how had she known the amount to make it out for if she hadn't made enquiries of the garage man? Of course she'd spoken to him; ridiculous to say it was Villana, ridiculous to say she'd sell the boarding-house tomorrow so as to be with him. She'd said that this afternoon. 'Oh my lovely soldier!' she'd said, her lips caressing his ear. She'd said something else, which he couldn't hear properly. More blandishments had followed, and then he thought she was suggesting she should become the cook at Carriglas before it dawned on him that she was again proposing to come to Carriglas as his wife. 'Mixed marriages are acceptable on my side,' she'd said, and unable to help himself he replied that it would be as suitable for him to marry one of the maids.

On the other lawn, across the gravel sweep, Villana picked up her brown-papered novel from the table beneath the strawberry trees. He watched her moving towards him and when she was close enough he offered her a cigarette, knowing she would not take one since she only smoked Craven A because of their cork tips. She walked beside him, among rosebushes that scented the evening air. Lionel would have to spare Haverty to tidy up the garden, she said. She did what she could and Sarah did what she could, but the garden could not be like this on the twenty-sixth.

'It's difficult with my leg,' he hastily interposed. 'I'd help if I could.'

'I didn't mean that.'

'I know you didn't.'

There was a silence. 'It's a burden,' his father had warned him once in Davison's Hotel. 'Any old place is a burden.' Finnamore Balt had a peculiar idea that various small-holdings should be obliged to yield their long-forgotten rents, that land should be repossessed. Finnamore Balt was keen to engage in litigation, even the litigation of eviction, offering his legal services free of charge. But that was something Lionel had shaken his head over also, and of course he was quite right: all it would mean was that the family would drown in a morass of quibbles and acrimony, every last ha'penny sucked out of what residue there was.

'Are you surprised that I am marrying?'

'Well yes, I have to say I am.'

He looked away, across the garden, feeling awkward. It was difficult to know what to say. It was difficult to voice any comment whatsoever, since the whole thing was an absurdity and since he had so much on his mind anyway. He wished he could tell her about his visits to the boarding-house, and how he couldn't rid himself of the feeling that he was being watched from beyond the grave. For a moment he considered telling her about the carpentry instructor's unprovoked attack on Asquith-Jones because he thought it might amuse her, but in the end he desisted. He heard her say there would be no children, but he didn't want to think about that and didn't listen to her voice when it continued. He would not return to the Rose of Tralee boarding-house, he resolved. As long as he lived he would never again find himself staring up at the bunches of lilies on the wallpaper.

5. Mr Coyne Changes His Mind

Tom's mother told him he had grandparents. There would be grandparents on his father's side, in Dublin somewhere: she had never known them, they had never been in touch with her. He had other grandparents, her own mother and father, living nine miles inland beyond the town. 'Your grandmother wants me to take you over one day.'

'Is my grandmother nice?'

'She is, Tom.'

'Is she like Mrs Rolleston at all?'

'She's half the age of Mrs Rolleston. Will we go over and see her?'

'We will.'

'I'll arrange it so.'

When there were holidays from the convent Tom's daytime world was the yard and the outhouses at Carriglas, and the sculleries, where he sometimes helped Patty to clean vegetables, and the fields, where sometimes he assisted Haverty. He roamed the island on his own, clambering down the cliffs to the rocks and the shrimp pools. He looked to see that the rosary crucifixes and the coins the women left at the holy well, on a ledge above the saint's pillow, remained undisturbed. He rarely climbed up to the standing stones.

'Mrs Rolleston wants you upstairs, Tom,' Patty said, coming to find him in the yard on the morning of the day he and his mother were to meet his grandmother. Overhearing

Patty's delivery of the summons, his mother said that Mrs Rolleston would have a message for him to do. 'If that's the way of it wait over there for me, Tom. Wait down on the quays till you'll see me coming.' Mrs Rolleston would give him twopence for himself, as she always did, and a penny for the ferry. He should spend the twopence on broken biscuits in Meath's, his mother said, and eat them while he was waiting.

'Fold the postal order, Tom,' Mrs Rolleston said in her bedroom. 'Then stick the envelope and put a stamp on it.'

'Fifteen shillings, is it?'

'Fifteen shillings. Don't lose the note now.'

He said he wouldn't, knowing he wouldn't because he never had, because there wasn't a hole in his trousers' pocket. 'I don't know what I'd do without you,' Mrs Rolleston said, but he knew she was only saying it. She was always nice like that, which was why he never minded going up to her bedroom.

'I'll tell you one thing,' the ferryman was saying on the ferry when Tom climbed on to it. 'Ireland was always famous for its bachelors.'

The ferryman hadn't started his engines yet. He was sitting on a side seat, where the passengers usually sat, beside one of the girls from Renehan's, who was conveying a basket of turkey eggs which she had placed on the boards at her feet. One of the girl's hands was bandaged, and Tom guessed she couldn't work in the fish sheds because of it. When the ferryman asked him, he had to confess he was uncertain about what a bachelor was.

'It's a man,' the ferryman said, 'that wouldn't have married a woman. D'you see that, boy? This lassie here has her eye on young Briscoe, only I'm after telling her that in my opinion Briscoe's the kind to remain a bachelor.'

Other bachelors were cited. The ferryman was a bachelor himself. So was Guard Ryan, and Sheehy in the coal yard, and Mr McGrath and Mr Tobin. Tom knew them all by sight. Sheehy always had a cigarette behind one of his ears. Guard Ryan was red-complexioned. Briscoe had white eyelashes and a broad flat face like a holy wafer. Mr McGrath and Mr Tobin were the two boarders in the Rose of Tralee boarding-house, Mr Tobin employed in the corn offices, Mr McGrath in the gasworks.

'I would have stated one time,' the ferryman ponderously continued, 'that Mr Balt was the kind to have remained a bachelor also, but I am proved mistaken.'

'Won't it be a great wedding?' interjected the girl. 'Is it soon, Tom?'

'On the twenty-sixth.'

The ferryman nodded his square, brown head. He was invited to the house, he said; he had not been forgotten. He'd heard Mr O'Hagan was assisting Haverty with the transport. 'Now, that's another bachelor we have. Mr O'Hagan. Are you going into the post office, Tom?'

'I am.'

'Will you tell Mr O'Hagan from me that Butt Nolan says hold back off Drummer's Lady?'

'I will.'

'Good man yourself.'

Nothing was said for a moment. Then the girl remarked that she had to leave the turkey eggs in at Dungan's and had half a stone of sugar to buy. She was the best-looking of the girls who went over to the fish sheds, Tom had always considered, even though she had a gangling stance when she stood up. She had bright white teeth and was always pushing her hair out of her eyes. Tom had heard the other girls teasing her about Briscoe, the bank porter.

'Take care with that fellow,' the ferryman advised her, and then he started the engines. In the usual way, no further conversation took place until the boat drew in at the quay, where Tom was reminded about the message for Mr O'Hagan. He walked along the quays with the girl, who explained that she had to go slowly in case she'd swing the basket and break one of the turkey eggs. 'I always wanted to ask you, Tom, only I couldn't because I wasn't alone with you. Does it feel like you'd be different?'

'I don't think it does,' he said.

'But if you would think about it, Tom? Would you feel different in yourself if you would think about it?'

'You don't feel anything at all.'

The girl lowered her voice. 'I once said a prayer for you, Tom.'

'There's no need for that.'

'Ah sure, I'd say a prayer for anyone. Sure, what does it cost me?' She turned into Dungan's grocery and Tom walked on. He felt in his pocket for the ten-shilling note and the extra coins. All the way over on the ferry and on his walk with the girl he'd been able to feel the corner of the envelope sticking into him in his other pocket. 'Hullo, Mr O'Hagan,' he said in the post office, and the post-office clerk regarded him as though he'd never seen him before. Nor did his expression change when eventually he spoke.

'Are you all right for yourself?'

'I am, Mr O'Hagan. I want a postal order for fifteen shillings.'

'I don't know have I one.'

'The ferryman says hold back off Drummer's Lady.'

Mr O'Hagan immediately ceased his search for the postal order. He looked hard at Tom, as though suspecting him of trickery. His face had lost some of its colour.

'Was it Butt Nolan told him that?'

'It was.'

'Did he mention anything else? Did he refer to Mister Fun?'

'He didn't.'

'I have money placed on Drummer's Lady. Isn't Nolan slow off the line on that one? Now, listen to me, young fellow. Go into Byrne's and ask for Mr O'Hagan's two shillings to be transferred off Drummer's Lady on to Mister

Fun. Will you remember those names now? Say them over to me.'

Tom repeated the racehorses' names. Mr O'Hagan nodded his satisfaction. With a swiftness that was unusual in him he supplied Tom with the postal order and told him to go quickly. 'Tell Mr Byrne I'd be down myself only I'm tied in behind the counter here.'

'Right you are, Mr O'Hagan.'

Tom folded the postal order into the envelope, stuck the envelope down and posted it. Then he walked down South Main Street to Byrne's the turf accountant's, where he explained that Mr O'Hagan's wager had gone on the wrong horse in error, that it should have been placed on Mister Fun. The man behind the counter released an incredulous guffaw. 'Will you listen to this?' he shouted through a door behind him, and caused a series of further guffaws in someone Tom couldn't see. 'Go back to the post office,' he instructed Tom, 'and ask Mr O'Hagan is he under the impression Artie Byrne was born in a pot?'

So Tom returned to the post office and had to wait behind a woman who was buying stamps for a parcel before he could put the question he'd been entrusted with to Mr O'Hagan. 'The old bags,' muttered Mr O'Hagan, at once becoming melancholy. Tom went quickly away before he was asked to return to the turf accountant's with some further plea, or a retaliation of abuse.

He bought a packet of lemonade powder in Buckley's, where the packets were bigger than the ones in Cush's or Barry's. He spilled it on to the palm of his hand and ate it walking along the street. He loitered outside Coyne's Garage in case Mr Coyne, who was filling a tin with petrol from his pump, had a message for the ferryman about a horse. 'How're you doing?' Mr Coyne enquired.

'I'm all right, Mr Coyne.' He told him about Drummer's Lady, how there'd been a warning from Butt Nolan only it hadn't reached Mr O'Hagan in time. He told him how Mr

O'Hagan had asked him to go into Byrne's and try to get the wager transferred to Mister Fun. Mr Coyne laughed, though not as heartily as Artie Byrne or the person Tom hadn't been able to see. 'I wouldn't consider either of those animals anything only doubtful,' Mr Coyne confided. 'To tell you the truth, there isn't an animal in that race I'd associate myself with.'

'I never saw horses racing, Mr Coyne.'

'You will one day, Tom. Maybe at Clonmel. Or Lismore. Did you ever see greyhounds?'

Tom shook his head.

'You have everything ahead of you so.'

'I heard you have a wireless set, Mr Coyne. They were saying it in the class one time.'

'They were right about that.'

'I never heard a wireless set yet.'

Having filled the tin with petrol, Mr Coyne was leaning against the pump. He began to say something; then Tom saw him changing his mind. He bent down to pick up the tin. Tom knew he'd been about to invite him to come into his house to hear his wireless set. 'I have work I must do,' he said instead.

So Tom walked on. He would have to tell his mother a lie if she asked about the broken biscuits, but she probably wouldn't. As he passed Traynor's Picture Palace, he wondered if he'd ever see a picture there. In the class the pictures that had been seen were sometimes talked about because Miss Welsh, the lay teacher, always wanted to know if anyone had gone to something good. *The Covered Wagon* was showing now.

'How're you, Tom?' Holy Mullihan said, and Tom had the same feeling Holy Mullihan always gave him: that he'd been waiting specially.

'I was out to see the bridge, Tom. Isn't it coming on grand?'

'It's good all right.'

'I was asking one of the priests the other day would it be blessed. Father Foyle, d'you know him? He's newly arrived with us.'

Tom shook his head. He'd never even heard of Father Foyle.

'The Bishop will come in to bless it, Tom. Every new building has to be blessed. Every room of a new house has to be sprinkled with holy water. Where're you going, Tom?'

'I'm hanging about. My mother's coming over on the ferry.'

'Wait till I'll tell you this. There was a saint, you wouldn't have heard of him, Tom, by the name of St Albert of Cashel. A great saint, Tom. There was a time St Albert was walking along a road and a certain type of woman came up to him. "I'd rather die where I'm standing," he said to her, "than have anything to do with you." She went down on her knees, Tom, and from that day out she changed her habits. Does your mother go to the well with the women, Tom?'

Tom said she did. Every year she went to the well when the date came round in August. Usually Tom went with her because she wanted him to. They'd gone this year.

'Did your mother ever go to Lough Derg or up Croagh Patrick, Tom? D'you know Croagh Patrick, Tom?'

'It's a mountain. We mark it in on the maps we do.'

Down a side street Tom caught a glimpse of the girl from the fish sheds. She was talking to Briscoe. She was swinging the basket she'd had the eggs in. Briscoe was leaning against the side of a house, with a cigarette going.

'You climb up Croagh Patrick on the last Sunday in July, Tom. There's a lot go on that pilgrimage. If a person wasn't at peace, or was in sin, the prayers made on the mountainside would uplift the soul. Father Foyle went one time, he was telling me. In the days before he entered the priesthood he was in doubt as regards his vocation. He found guidance on holy Croagh Patrick, Tom.'

Holy Mullihan then told a story about St Cronan of

Roscrea, after which he outlined the death of St Peter Martyr. 'D'you know what it is, didn't he dip his finger in the blood that came out of his head and didn't he write in the dust with it? *Credo in Deum*, Tom. Then he was hit another blow.'

Holy Mullihan crossed himself. All the time he was talking, Tom thought about Mr Coyne and how he had changed his mind about inviting him into his house. 'My father said to keep distant from you,' a girl in the class had said, Dorrie Deavy it was. Another girl had said the same. It was maybe that if he'd gone into the house one of the Coyne girls would have stood too near him when they were listening to the wireless set, or even tried to take his hand, not knowing.

'There's stories you'd hear that wouldn't be true, Tom. There's one relating to St Cronan, where St Cronan performed a miracle in order to extend the amount of stout they had in the monastery and the result was the whole crowd of them got drunk. There's not a word of truth in that, Tom. If you'd ever hear it repeated contradict the whole thing.'

Tom said he would.

'D'you ever think of Father Quirke, Tom? I thought of him that night when we attended the knife-throwing. It was the intention that Father Quirke's park would be a place where people could rest themselves. What happened was, there was a big disaster in America and the poor man who gave us the bit of land got left without a penny. I often tell that story to illustrate a point I'd have to make. D'you know much about Father Quirke, Tom?'

Tom shook his head.

'He carried temperance with him, Tom. The temperance was like a path he made. As soon as it's suitable, Tom, take a pledge that you won't ever consume strong drink. You'll be the better man for it.'

Holy Mullihan gave a sideways wag of his head. There

was a little booklet about Father Quirke which he'd lend Tom the next time he saw him. It told about his boyhood in the poor part of the town and how he'd seen a man falling down after drink at the top of Michael Davitt Hill, only it hadn't been called that in those days. He had taken the pledge himself, Holy Mullihan said, and was the better for it. There was never stout in a monastery, he said, which was how you'd know the story about St Cronan was made up.

'Father Quirke would have walked where we're walking now, Tom. We could be going in his footsteps.'

'Was it the truth when you said people mightn't like to touch me?'

There were small pimples around Holy Mullihan's mouth, some of them almost obscured by the growth of soft hair that flourished there also. The tips of his fingers investigated these before he began to reply. He pursed his lips into a knot. He said:

'It's a thing that isn't easy to explain, Tom. It's like a stain you'd carry on you. Like you'd get a stain on a garment. There's a thing called contamination, Tom, which these people would be worried about.' Holy Mullihan paused. He pointed in the direction of the Church of Our Lady. 'Will we go inside?'

Tom said there wouldn't be time. Any minute now his mother would be arriving on the ferryboat. He had promised to be ready.

'D'you ever think about Our Lady, Tom?' Not waiting for an answer, Holy Mullihan recited the great feasts that had to be kept in the Virgin's name: the Annunciation, the Assumption, her Birthday, her Immaculate Conception, her Immaculate Heart, her Motherhood, her Presentation, her Purification, her Sorrows, her Visit to Elizabeth. 'Say them off to your mother, Tom. Tell your mother about Croagh Patrick, Tom.'

'I will.'

'I'll be seeing you so.'

Tom went away quickly. He'd once gone into the church with Holy Mullihan and they'd knelt there for ages. Holy Mullihan had done everything slowly, taking the holy water, crossing himself, making his obeisance. He'd knelt in a special way, a bone sticking out of the back of his neck when he bent it in prayer. He'd asked Tom if he'd any money so that they could light a candle, but Tom hadn't.

On the quays Tom stood in the doorway of a warehouse. He could see the boat just beginning its journey and he watched it making its way across, people stepping off it and the returning travellers being greeted by the ferryman. When it had drawn out into the water he went to the quayside and sat on a bollard. The ferryman never talked to his mother the way he did to the girls from the fish sheds or to the other passengers. Going over with her to Mass on Sundays, Tom had noticed it, and he noticed it when she arrived now: she was the only passenger, and when the engines were turned off the ferryman didn't begin a conversation. His mother had the stain too, was what Holy Mullihan had meant.

Together, they walked from the quays. Neck Daly and Deso Furphy were picking at the paint blisters on the shutters of the closed-up shop in South Main Street, and Tom hoped they'd call across the street to him so that he could tell his mother who they were – older boys who were already at the Brothers', who even so would bother to address him. But they didn't see him, nor did Father Pierce, who was going into Barry's. Tom had never before gone to the promenade with his mother, which was where she said they were going now, although he'd thought they would be walking out to his grandmother's house. They passed the hall-doors with the brass plates. Ikely the dentist had a nickname in the class, he told his mother. 'Feathery Ike,' he said.

His mother was hurrying and distracted, not interested in the nickname. There was a rhyme that went with it:

Feathery Ike, Feathery Ike, give us a ride on your buttery bike. He hadn't understood it until Neck Daly explained it had been made up because the dentist bore a resemblance to a parrot, and because a pound of butter had once melted in the basket on his bicycle. Sister Teresa Dolores had had a tooth drawn by him once and it wouldn't stop bleeding. She'd had to keep a towel in her mouth all night.

'Hullo,' his mother said to a woman in a black shawl. The woman had seen them approaching her and had risen from the promenade seat where she'd been sitting. 'Well, is that Tom?' she said. He thought she was going to kiss him but she didn't.

She was a slight woman, with grey hair hardly showing under the edge of her shawl. 'You're looking well, Brigid,' she said.

'You're looking well yourself.'

'I have my health, thank God, Brigid.'

'Did you walk it in?'

'I did walk it. I came on the back road. It's better the back way.'

'It is.'

The conversation ceased. The shawled woman examined Tom closely. After a while she said:

'Is a weekday hard for you with your work?'

'I can fix it.'

'He'd know what I'd be up to on a Sunday. I'd be frightened he'd follow me.'

'Is he the same about it?'

'He'll always be the same about it.'

For a long time the two women again sat in silence. The promenade was crowded, an excursion train having recently arrived. New powder pictures had been completed on the sand, peacocks in a garden, a waterfall and a glen. The elderly man who created them was just beginning another, skilfully working his garish powders. Tom drew his mother's attention to them, but she hardly looked.

'Tom looks after the holy well,' she said. 'He was asked would he do it by Father Pierce.'

'Father Pierce was good to you, Brigid.' She'd never visited the well, she said to Tom; she'd never been over on the island. 'I've heard tell it has holy clay.'

'You can feel it wet in your fingers.'

'Tom felt it often,' his mother said, and from the tone of her voice Tom knew she was telling his grandmother this so that his grandmother could understand he benefited from the holiness of the well. She'd always been eager herself for him to look after it. 'Father Pierce was on about you,' she'd said. 'I told him you didn't neglect the well.' When Father Pierce had arranged with Mrs Rolleston that he should go to the convent nobody had said it was on account of it being necessary for him to be near the holiness of the nuns, but he knew now that was what Father Pierce and his mother considered.

'It's good you look after the well,' his grandmother said. 'That's grand for me to know.'

Without warning she wept.

Tom turned away and gazed over the sea at the island, at the grey bulk of Carriglas, and the green hillsides speckled with yellow. The distress continued beside him. The latest picture on the sand was of a woman holding a bunch of flowers. He watched while colour was smeared over a tulip. His mother's voice murmured consolation.

'Dear Mother of God,' his grandmother sobbed, struggling with the words. 'Dear Mary forgive you, Brigid.'

*

He didn't arrive. She waited until a quarter to five, worrying in case the ferry had sunk. A dozen times she looked from her window but the boat was still chugging back and forth, every hour or so. He must be suffering from something, she thought in the end, summer 'flu or stomach. Carefully, yet again, she went over his visit of a week ago. There hadn't been a word between them. He'd come out with only a single one of his hurtful remarks, not that he ever intended to cause pain, inexperience really.

She worried, knowing it was unreasonable to do so. She worried because it had never happened before, because ever since they'd made the Monday arrangement he'd kept to it, in spite of his boyish touchiness. She always thought of him as a boy, she couldn't help it. 'My soldier boy,' she'd said the first day, when he'd come in to listen to *Get Along, Little Doggy* on the gramophone. She'd been sorry for him, so young with his limp. When he'd come back another time he'd told her the details of the wound he'd sustained, still downstairs they were in those days. He'd told her about some other poor fellow who'd had the side of his face affected by shrapnel from a shell.

At five o'clock she heard sounds downstairs, but knew it was only the maid returning after her free afternoon. He wouldn't come now; he wouldn't even come in to explain in case he'd be seen by the boarders. He'd refused to take a cheque in any shape or form, so during the week she'd got the money out of the Munster and Leinster and the fellow, Corcoran, had the neck to be inquisitive about it. Ignorant lump of a fellow, telling her not to leave it lying around.

She dressed. She had seven to cook for. Bacon and eggs and fried tomatoes, a sausage each. Two pots of tea, one for McGrath and Tobin, the other for the family of five from Dunmanway. Tinned pineapple afterwards for the family of five, but McGrath and Tobin wouldn't be bothered with that. The other houses did something extra for the families, so she'd taken to it herself, something they'd remember. She'd been explaining about that to him the last time, how she liked to offer pineapple pieces or jelly or a jellycream, or a slice of a Scribbin's Swiss roll if she hadn't anything else to hand. She'd kept to subjects like that because the other had given him a shock, but of course you couldn't not mention for ever something that was close to you. If the sister could turn round and marry a string of fish like Balt, the subject could surely be at least raised. The sister was doing it for money, no argument about that; without in any way rushing him into it she'd endeavoured to make it clear that she did not intend to come empty-handed herself.

Maybe he'd had to go to Cork on the train because a necessity for the sister's wedding hadn't arrived. Or he could have tripped over something that was in an unusual place because of the preparations; he could have injured his bad leg. Mrs Moledy straightened the bedclothes and looked out of the window. The sister's bridegroom went by on the promenade, the family from Dunmanway were sitting on a seat. No point in fretting, though it was hard not to: six days would have to go by before she'd know. The banknotes were in the hat-box on top of the wardrobe, underneath the tissue paper and the hat she'd worn the day she'd got married herself, cordial-green with a veil, hardly ever taken out now.

Supposing he never came again? Supposing he'd met some Protestant girl and gone for her? You might be standing in Dungan's and you'd hear about it, the way you always heard about things in shops. One of the Blenner-hassett girls, or one of the Garlands. He'd go with her, having scattered his wild oats, forgetting altogether that he was loved, that his face stayed behind long after he went away on a Monday. She'd told him he was good-looking. She'd told him other things too, but what he'd never understood was how there'd be nothing left of her if he didn't come any more. She'd said that to him maybe twenty times on a Monday, first thing and last in spite of any words they'd have. But his eyes were sometimes listless, as if the pain in his wound had come on.

Agitated by her thoughts, Mrs Moledy blew her nose and powdered away the smears on her cheeks. She descended to the hall, and having opened the door that led down to the kitchen, she shouted to her maid, who she knew would be reluctant to get on with anything until she appeared herself. She'd be gone five minutes, she called down, and then hurried out to Myley Flynn's, for the drink she felt in need of.

*

Carriglas, August 22nd, 1931. The wedding-cake arrived today, from Thompson's in Cork. Miss Laffey, who has constantly been over to take fittings, sent word to say she has completed the dress. We again aired the visitors' rooms. Brigid came upstairs to polish because Patty is still slow, and Mrs Haverty works morning and afternoon now. There will be six to stay, and almost fifty on the wedding day.

At dinner tonight there was talk of the bridge, though the subject of the memorial inscription was not touched upon.

'I would almost wager,' John James declared, 'that some calamity of engineering will befall that bridge. Before it's completed the structure will collapse and will not after-wards be resumed.'

'Why on earth should that be?' his grandmother demanded, prompting him to cite examples of abandoned projects in the past: a road in Co. Mayo that was washed away when it was half constructed, a tramway there was to have been in Limerick.

Villana contributed an observation to the conversation; Lionel none. 'A statue of O'Connell,' John James con-tinued, 'was planned one time for Clonakilty. To be cast in bronze, only they lost the middle part of it and poor O'Connell came out a dwarf.'

Villana laughed: that was so, she agreed, she had heard the statue talked about. Lionel still said nothing. It sur-prised me that I had never heard in Bandon this story of Clonakilty's statue, the two towns being close to one another. But I did not remark on that.

After dinner I took the ironing to the first-floor hot-press, and then completed my evening tasks in the kitchen. Patty remained for a while, reading Ireland's Own at the table after Brigid had gone down to the gate-lodge; then she said goodnight. I repaired some pillowslips that would be needed for the visitors. I waited, the kettle boiling on the range, but when Lionel came in he said he was tired tonight and would go to bed at once.

I feel more than ever that I live in a cobweb of other people's lives and do not understand the cobweb's nature. These are the people I knew as children; this is the same house; trees and shrubs are as they were. I remind myself of that when everywhere I sense what I can only call distortion; I know no better word. I tell myself that John James suffers from his wounded leg, that it's his brother's choice to live a peasant's life, that other girls have married sticks for husbands.

I tell myself, but I feel as though I'm telling lies. The old woman sits austerely at the dinner table, preserving with them a privacy they hardly deign to recognise. I am not worthy of whatever secret there is, only good for the chores a poor relation must take on as her due. 'The place would fall to pieces after I've gone,' the old woman said the day I came back. 'Thank you for returning, Sarah.' But at dinner and in the drawing-room I feel trapped by my own weakness, more than ever I was trapped in the boarding-school or in my father's rectory. I should leave Carriglas, but I cannot find the courage.

6. Visitors on the Island

Tom delighted in the kitchen's turmoil. He kept out of the way, but was allowed to be in the kitchen or its vicinity in case there were errands to be run or a task which might be allocated to him. The house – until recently a wonder to him – became familiar that summer. He carried to the hot-press beside the first-floor bathroom the tins of meringues and brandysnaps and wafer biscuits that had been made. He peeped into rooms when the doors were open – the drawing-room and the dining-room, the breakfast room where the fire smoked, the small study. No one ever asked him where he was going or what he was doing when someone else had commissioned a chore; he did not speak unless he was addressed, which was not often; he felt he was not noticed.

In the sculleries he was allowed to assist Patty and Mrs Haverty with the washing and drying of china that Mrs Haverty said hadn't been used for years, to judge from the dust on it. He told Patty about the time the cloths hanging above the range had caught fire, and how a storm had blown the slates off the gate-lodge and Haverty had to climb up and replace them. Once a man had come over on the ferry to repair the banister-rail, and he'd knocked at the gate-lodge door to ask if he was in the right place. 'Show him the way up the avenue,' Tom's mother had said, which was the first time Tom had ever done anything like that. Five he was then.

For her part, Patty said, if she'd mended one tablecloth she'd mended forty, and confided to Tom that she was exhausted. The wedding lunch was to be laid out on what would seem to be a single long table when it was disguised by the tablecloths, with baize beneath them. Haverty had already arranged the trestles on the lawn bordered by delphinium beds, which was conveniently close to the dining-room French windows. Chairs had been brought from all over the house, some of them by Tom. 'Would you marry that fellow?' Patty whispered in the sculleries. 'I wouldn't if he'd won the Sweep.'

Spread out on the kitchen table, silver was cleaned – teapots and trays, cutlery, jugs and gravy boats, embossed napkin-rings, fish knives worn so thin they were almost sharp. In the yard Mrs Haverty beat rugs and carpets. The sideboard door in the dining-room was repaired, a blocked-up lavatory seen to. There was concern about what would happen if the fish went off in the heat, and Tom's mother said there'd always be the ham to fall back on. Mrs Haverty agreed to kill a few chickens.

Then the first of the visitors arrived. Tom waited with Haverty at the pier, and a man and a woman stepped off the ferryboat and the ferryman handed their suitcases to Haverty. The visitors took their places in the trap. Tom led the horse as Haverty had instructed him, Haverty himself following with the luggage in a cart. The man and the woman laughed and chattered, and when they came to the avenue the woman said she hadn't been through the gates of Carriglas for thirty-one years. 'What's your name?' the man called out to him, and he said it was Tom. 'You're a good boy, Tom,' the woman said, and Tom heard her whispering to the man to be sure to give him a threepenny-piece. But when they arrived at the house the man forgot about that.

A clergyman came in the same manner, with his wife, who was a cousin of the late Colonel Rolleston, Haverty said. Tom knew what Colonel Rolleston had looked like from the photograph on the table in the hall, but the woman who was his cousin didn't have a similar appearance, being as rotund as he'd been tall, her neck lost in the spreading flesh of her chins. The clergyman was severe, his bald head not tanned like the ferryman's nor pinkly gleaming like Mr Coyne's: it looked like suet. It was he who would conduct the marriage service, Haverty said, on account of being connected with the family. In the trap this couple did not laugh and chatter as the others had. They didn't ask Tom his name.

A woman with a faded face came. She had hair that was faded to a nondescript greyness, and faded clothes, but her voice was different from the rest of her, being shrill and most determined. 'Can that boy manage?' she sharply questioned Haverty. 'Suppose the horse bolts?'

In the trap she continued to exclaim, shrieking at Tom to take care of the pot-holes. She held on her knees a parcel she had refused to be parted from, a wedding present of great fragility. 'Something's up with this place,' she commented as they approached the avenue gates. 'They've let it go.' Then she called out that the horse should be made to progress more slowly. 'Show me where they murdered the butler,' she peremptorily commanded, and Tom did, when they came to the spot.

Some time later a young man with glasses arrived and was similarly conveyed. He wore a long black overcoat and a woollen scarf in spite of the heat of the day, and having settled himself into the trap, wrapped a travelling rug around his knees. He told Haverty it had been very expensive for him to come to the wedding, since he'd been obliged to travel from well beyond Athlone, where he was at present staying with an uncle. Young men like that stayed a lot in relations' houses, Haverty afterwards explained to Tom. The couple who'd arrived first were the Camiers from Unionhall, he said; before their marriage she might have been a Pollexfen, the better-off branch of that family, he wasn't sure. The clergyman was the Protestant Bishop of Killaloe. The faded woman was Lady Rossboyne.

Two more traps, and the dog-cart and the governess-car, were to be drawn by the farm horses and a pony on the day of the wedding, so that all these visitors and the Rollestons themselves could be accommodated on the journey to the pier. Tom helped Haverty to wash down the governess-car and the dog-cart in the yard, and then Haverty pushed them about, steering them with their shafts, to make sure the wheels didn't continue to squeak after he'd greased them. It had been arranged that Mr O'Hagan would drive the dog-cart on the day of the wedding, and Lionel and John James would take a trap each. He'd take the third trap himself. 'Would you manage the governess-car?' he suggested to Tom. 'Come down on the avenue and I'll show you.'

Tom, who had learnt the day before how to lead a horse by the bridle, now learnt how to hold the reins and control the pace of the governess-car pony. 'I'll be in front of you,' Haverty said. 'Just keep her steady.' When the instruction was over, the pony was allowed to graze on the verge of the avenue and Haverty lit a cigarette and told Tom about a regatta there had been, the last occasion when there'd been as much company at Carriglas as there would be on the wedding day. Yachts and sailing-boats had raced around the island; boats had come up from Dunmore East and Dungarvan; there'd been different coloured sails, and flags along the quaysides. In the evening some of the boats had come in at the old landing-stage and everyone had gone up to the house to make a night of it. Well before the war it would have been, maybe 1905.

Because his mother didn't have time to go down to the gate-lodge that evening, she fried Tom slices of griddle bread in the kitchen of the house and made him his cocoa there. Patty came in with the slender-stemmed glasses she'd been sent to collect from the drawing-room, from which sherry had been drunk. 'God, wouldn't that crowd frighten the life out of you?' she whispered to Tom.

*

The visitors so observed and remarked upon in turn observed and remarked upon the bridegroom, since none of them had met Finnamore Balt before. Invited to dinner at Carriglas on the first evening of their stay, he was mistaken by Lady Rossboyne for someone else, and in her forthright manner she said so several times before the matter was set right. The Bishop was equally taken aback, having been unaware that his wife's young relative had become engaged to a man so very much her senior. His wife, he could divine from her expression, had been unaware also.

Mrs Camier of Unionhall was particularly surprised, for although she and her husband had known that Finnamore was an older man, she had not been prepared for the austerity of his appearance and a manner that suggested to her some inner discomfort – possibly digestive troubles. Money must come into it, her husband privately remarked to her as the party moved from the drawing-room to the dining-room. Only the young man with glasses, whose name was Villiers Hadnett, found nothing unusual about Villana's bridegroom, being mainly interested in himself.

In the dining-room Patty was nervous with the dishes, even though Brigid had warned her that she mustn't be. Mrs Haverty carried trays, but advanced into the room no further than the sideboard. 'Didn't you replace your butler?' Lady Rossboyne enquired, noting the rudimentary nature of these arrangements. 'Very grand we all thought you, having a butler.'

'We hadn't the heart to replace him,' Mrs Rolleston replied from her end of the table. 'And then time went on and we couldn't afford to.'

'Well, I never! Did you hear that, Bishop?'

'I beg your pardon, Lady Rossboyne?'

But Lady Rossboyne chose not to supply the Bishop with the information she had drawn his attention to. Instead she related how she herself had been fortunate to escape unharmed on an occasion during the Troubles, when a tar barrel had been set alight in the room beneath the one where she was sleeping. The neighbouring Buttevant Court, as no doubt was well known, had been razed to the ground.

'We were mercifully overlooked,' the Bishop murmured, but Lady Rossboyne did not wish to hear the details of that. The child with the governess-car had shown her where the outrage had occurred. She'd naturally asked about it.

'Linchy was his father,' Mrs Rolleston said.

'That child's father? So Linchy was a married man?'

'He wasn't. But that didn't stop him from taking our parlourmaid into his bed.'

'Good Lord!'

'Brigid's come up in the world since then. She cooked the fish you're eating.'

'You mean you kept her on?'

'She would hardly have cooked the fish if we hadn't.'

'So that child ...' the Bishop began, and did not continue.

'Kings of England have come into the world so,' Mrs Rolleston said. 'Kings of Ireland too, no doubt.'

The visitors, intrigued by what they'd heard, consumed their fish in silence. Then John James mentioned the bridge, offering a fresh topic of conversation. Long anticipated, he reported, the work had begun in the spring.

'A bridge?' repeated the Bishop. 'I did not know this.' He frowned severely. First there was the elderly bridegroom, then a child illegitimately born to servants, now the information that the island was to change its nature. The Bishop glanced at his wife and saw that she, too, continued to be nonplussed. A necklace of garnets, inherited a year ago, decorated the folds of her neck and was the only sign of life about her, for her features had gone blank and her knife and fork lay still on the plate in front of her. He had witnessed this before when she suffered bewilderment.

'Girders,' John James said, 'are already set in cement.'

The Camiers had observed the understructure from the ferry and had remarked to one another that a bridge appeared to be in the process of construction. Villiers Hadnett had noticed nothing. Nor had Lady Rossboyne.

'This is truly singular,' the Bishop declared, raising his voice so that it would carry to his wife and rouse her. She gave a little jerk and dutifully turned to Lionel to talk about her children. 'Our older son's in India,' she said. 'Managing a tea plantation.'

If people would like it, John James suggested, tomorrow they might walk across the island to see what progress the bridge was making. He observed that a feature of life nowadays in Ireland was that little was brought to completion. He mentioned the Limerick tramway and the loss of the middle section of Daniel O'Connell's statue. He drew attention to the plans there'd once been for a park in memory of a temperance priest.

'But we might see for ourselves,' he suggested. 'If that would be agreeable.'

His mind was not on what he said. A letter had come from her, a thing that had never occurred before. She had apparently withdrawn from the bank the price of the motor-car in ten-pound notes. There was something he couldn't read properly, about a hat-box, and tissue paper, and about being nervous because there was a family from Dunmanway in the house, people she'd never laid eyes on till a week ago. He'd torn the whole rigmarole up, envelope and all, and gone specially to the kitchen to burn the pieces in the range since there was no other fire in August.

'I had not heard about a bridge,' the Bishop repeated. 'We neither of us had heard a word about a bridge.'

Villiers Hadnett, regarding the surface of the table in front of him, spoke to Mrs Camier of his journey from Athlone. Finding this tedious, Mrs Camier turned to Finnamore, who was on her other side. 'You're in the law, Mr Balt?' she said.

'Yes, I am in the law,' Finnamore replied. 'I have been a solicitor all my life.'

'And is that agreeable?'

Finnamore gave the question his consideration. He knew about the Camiers. They had run through a great deal of money. Camier, before this present marriage, had been sued for breach of promise. Mrs Camier was pretty and presented an air of flightiness. She was said to pride herself on being able to draw people out.

'I do not complain,' Finnamore said. 'I believe I never have. On the other hand, I know no other work.'

'Now, though, if you had a choice, Mr Balt,' pursued Mrs Camier in a kittenish manner, her eyelids blinking rapidly. 'If you could choose from all the world's work, what would you say?'

Finnamore considered that question carefully also. He pondered, chewing a fragment of vegetable, before replying. He thought to smile, but did not do so, fearing Mrs Camier might interpret this as a lack of serious attention paid to her query.

'I believe I would run the same course,' he finally pronounced. 'I cannot see myself tempted elsewhere.'

'Not travel and adventure? Not the dash and thrill of commerce?'

'I think not. I am familiar with the law. I know nothing of commercial matters.'

Mrs Camier, sensing that the conversation she had worked so hard to stimulate was about to dry up, and reluctant to be again exposed to the continuing monologue of Villiers Hadnett's journey from Athlone, touched Finnamore lightly on the arm with the tips of her fingers and said she could easily see him adventuring in Africa – a claim that visibly startled the solicitor. Not understanding that Mrs Camier was seeking to set a carefree mood, he wondered why she had poked him with her fingers. It was unusual at dinner, he considered, for a woman to behave so; it seemed to him unusual, also, for a woman to keep opening and closing her eyes so much. Her husband, he noticed, was drinking a great deal of wine – which, if he only knew it, the Rollestons could ill afford. Mr Camier issued a short, barking laugh from time to time but did not speak much.

'I have never considered life in Africa,' he said. 'I am not that kind of person.'

'Then tell me, Mr Balt, what kind of a person you would say you were. Tell me without thinking. Say straight out. Lower your voice if you feel the need to.'

Further down the table, the Bishop's wife spoke about her second son, who, in spite of not possessing his brother's advantages, was also doing well, having established himself in Jacob's Biscuits, where he was in charge of an accounting room. 'At school he did the sums in his head. Never wrote a figure down.' The Bishop's wife nodded in support of her claim, disturbing a little the garnets on the folds of her neck as she did so. Lionel said he often ate Jacob's biscuits.

'So, you see, it is the year of the bridge.' Re-filling the wine-glasses, John James endeavoured to keep things going on the other side of the table. 'We shall remember 1931 as that. The bridge that never was, I'd lay a wager.'

'I should have thought, more likely, as the year of Villana's wedding,' the Bishop corrected.

'That too,' John James willingly conceded. 'Villana's wedding.'

Lionel's thoughts, also, were far removed from the conversation he engaged in. So were Villana's. Mrs Moledy's naked body had now entered John James's and would not go away.

'I think I am a serious person,' Finnamore said in reply to further pressure from Mrs Camier. 'I think I am a person who takes things seriously. I was a serious child. I have a serious disposition.'

'And nothing else to add, eh?'

Patty said to herself that any moment now she would spill either the mint sauce or the gravy. Mrs Haverty, alert by the door, thought she could have efficiently assisted with the peas and the potatoes, and felt cross that she had not been asked. She had managed to fit into the uniform that had been worn by a maid of similar size in the past; it seemed hard that she was not permitted to advance further than the sideboard.

'When Villana and I are married I am to live at Carriglas,' Finnamore informed his interlocutor in an effort to alter the nature of the conversation. 'That has been agreed between us because Villana wishes it, because Villana has lived here all her life. Well, of course I am delighted,' Finnamore went on, taking pleasure in his revelations now. 'But I had seriously to consider the fate of my cat and my maid. I did not ask my maid to accompany me, and Villana has a fear of cats.'

'I should have thought the extra help of your maid might have been welcomed.'

'It would be alien for her here. She is no longer young and was a boon companion of my mother's. No, it is better not so. My clerk, Eugene Prille, has found good homes for both of them.'

'Prille?'

'That is the name of my clerk.'

'Well, that's most interesting. *Most* interesting. It is not a name I am familiar with.' Mrs Camier paused, and then continued: 'It's a wrench to be parted from a pet. You'll find it so?'

'Indeed. Prille is a Huguenot name originally. Eugene passed his childhood in Macroom.'

'Mr Balt, there is something you are not telling me, I think!'

'Well, only perhaps that when I come to Carriglas I shall be closer to the condition of the estate. It is a dream, shared with Villana, that between us we may return Carriglas to its former glory.'

'Now how very nice that sounds!'

'Due in part to generosity and in part to negligence, much is in need of attention. There is land that must be winkled back to the family. I, with knowledge of such matters, will perhaps devote my life to that. I do not know if you're aware of the history of this family? In particular of the generation we call the Famine Rollestons?'

'I think not.'

'The John Rolleston of that time married Catherine Esmond of Ninemilecross. It was they who first of all waived the rents.'

'How odd of them!'

'People had perished all around them. If they had not died of starvation they poisoned themselves with the weeds they ate. The Famine Rollestons were widely renowned for their compassion. A most remarkable generation, but alas disastrous in terms of the effect on the family fortunes.'

'Well, that's most interesting.' Mrs Camier's encouraging murmur suddenly acquired an acerbic note; her eyelids ceased their motion. She had herself once contemplated marriage for money: she could not recall if the price had seemed as high. Hastily she returned her attention to Villiers Hadnett, who was now revealing details concerning his state of health.

'So she's not to marry Hugh Pollexfen?' Lady Rossboyne said loudly and in a general way.

'No.' It was Lionel who replied, being close by.

'The engagement was broken off more than ten years ago,' Mrs Rolleston called down the table.

'At Buttevant we made sure it was Hugh Pollexfen.

The present I brought had Hugh Pollexfen in mind.'

'Villana is to marry Mr Balt,' Mr Camier explained.

'Of course she is. They told us in the drawing-room. What I'm saying is why not Hugh Pollexfen?'

'A disagreement, I dare say,' Mr Camier hazarded, and gave one of his short laughs. 'Presumably they were unsuited.'

Lady Rossboyne was not entirely satisfied by that. The couple would not have become engaged in the first place if they were unsuited, she pointed out. She had taken the bridegroom they'd been presented with to be Hugh Pollexfen's uncle, one of the Pollexfens of Rosscarbery. She found the circumstances bizarre.

'Of course it is often the case,' the Bishop confided to Mrs Rolleston, 'that a singular match turns out to be one of the most profound happiness.' The severity of his eyes deepened, affected by a mood of earnestness. 'I have observed it often in my experience.'

'I, on the contrary, have not. I quite deplore all this.'

'Deplore?'

'This wedding is an occasion of farce.'

Aghast, the Bishop made a sound he had not intended to, caused by the onset of alarm. Food hurried down his throat. His jaw sagged.

'I have come to conduct the wedding,' he said, realising as he spoke that the words were foolish.

'You may recall you wrote to ask if you might.'

'I do indeed recall. It seemed a friendly move to make. A wedding within the family. I am a bishop, after all.'

'Villana was touched. She shares with you this family thing.'

'I had no idea you disapproved.'

'It is not disapproval. Disapproval is a different sentiment entirely. It is simply that I yet have hopes Villana may draw back.'

'In what way draw back? What do you mean?'

'I mean that, faced with the ultimate before the altar, Villana will walk away from it. I really cannot see that she'll fail to realise in time.'

'But this is no way to begin a marriage. They have vows to make. I shall be speaking to both of them. I was quite unaware there was some doubt.'

'I had a dream that Villana said she was destroying the poor man's peace of mind.'

'A dream?'

'Take no notice of me. I believe the feeling is that I am ga-ga. I believe that's so.'

'Oh, surely – '

'Being ga-ga is seeing things differently when you're old. How horrid this trifle is!'

She would give a shilling, the Bishop's wife thought, to be able to go away and take off her stays. 'Scarlatina,' Villiers Hadnett said. 'And trouble with a lung.' Mr Camier again drained his glass and gave another laugh. It was odd, Lady Rossboyne mused, that the bridegroom should have reminded her of the original bridegroom's uncle. Mrs Rolleston stood up.

In the drawing-room there was coffee, and then the men came in after they had sat over their port for half an hour. Lady Rossboyne and Mrs Rolleston talked about the past; mutual relatives were recalled. Mrs Camier attempted to draw out Lionel and did not succeed. While listening to Villiers Hadnett telling him about his lung, John James remembered the name of the carpentry instructor: Spokeshave Billimore. Finnamore supplied Mr Camier with the history of the Ganters, from Kanturk, who had briefly had a connection with the Rollestons. His partner, Harbinson, was to be his best man, he informed Mr Camier. The Harbinsons were originally of Mountmellick.

Mrs Camier, drawing out the Bishop, heard about ten minutes that had changed his life. Ten minutes in May 1894, a Tuesday morning. The bells of St Canice's cathedral in Kilkenny had been ringing at the time, but Mrs Camier was never to discover why, because while the Bishop was explaining how he had grappled with a theological enigma during those particular ten minutes the evening was brought to an end. 'Goodnight,' Mrs Rolleston abruptly said, and taking from his waistcoat the watch Villana had liked to play with as a child, Finnamore noted that it was almost the time he had arranged for the ferryman to be at the pier. The double journey was to cost him a price he considered high: one and sixpence because of the lateness of the hour. He shook hands with the visitors; Villana accompanied him from the drawing-room.

'Lady Rossboyne is very direct,' she apologised on the avenue. 'I'm sorry.'

'She did not offend me.'

Villana took his arm. He was so very kind, coming to Carriglas when he might have insisted on remaining in his house, obliging her to live where she did not wish to live. The interest he took in Carriglas was a kindness also: she saw it as such.

'But I fear I did not make much impression.' He sighed. One way or another he had not enjoyed the evening. He had made no headway in his conversation with Mrs Camier; and her husband had finally interrupted him to say he had no interest in genealogy. 'They found me dull and much too old for you.'

'It does not matter what they found you. That is of no importance.'

Again he sighed. He could not help wishing his reception had been warmer; it was a natural thing.

'Finny, will you be nice to me about something?'

'Yes, my dear. Of course.'

'There is no real need to make a fuss about the inscription on the bridge.'

He stopped in his walk, considerably taken aback.

'Oh, but there is. I have put the case forcibly. No one has been left in doubt.'

'Funds for the inscription have already been collected. It is always difficult to reverse such decisions.'

'But not impossible. We have reason on our side. We have humane considerations.'

'We would rather you did not continue to make a fuss.'

'But, my dear little girl – '

'I believe I speak for all of us. The bridge is there, and that is that. John James pretends it will somehow not be completed, but of course we know it will be. Similarly with the memorial plaque.'

'That man sought to murder you and your brothers. In a most gruesome manner he brought to an end the life of an unfortunate servant.'

'Yes, I know.'

'He chose to be the family's enemy. Had he lived he would have burnt Carriglas to the ground.'

'Yes, that is probably true.'

'Every time you cross that bridge – '

'We know about every time, Finny. We are well aware. But we would rather you did not make a fuss.'

He made no further comment. In silence they continued through the gloom.

*

After their journeys the visitors retired early that night. The Camiers, who had accepted the wedding invitation because of the lavishness of the Carriglas parties they'd heard spoken about, consoled themselves with a decanter surreptitiously conveyed to their bedroom. Villiers Hadnett pulled the bell in the wall by his bed, requiring a carafe of water, but no one came. The Bishop confided to his wife that he was greatly perturbed by the prediction that Villana at the last minute would draw back from the altar and he himself be made to look a fool. His wife, involved at that moment with her stays, replied that she would not be in the very least surprised. Lady Rossboyne's mattress, in the past lain upon by the Viceroy during his summer visits, had become lumpy with the passing of time. 'No better than turnips in a sack,' she crossly muttered.

*

Carriglas, August 25th, 1931. This morning John James set up the croquet hoops, and the game was played again, as I remember it in the past. Afterwards the visitors sat beneath the strawberry trees or strolled about. Their presence dominates the household, and has become its centre, even though Villana is the reason for their being here. John James makes what effort he can. Yet neither he nor Villana – and certainly not their brother – seems able to escape from the shadows of their abandoned lives. More than ever I recall the trinity they formed as children, when only my brother was invited to share its secrets. I cannot help believing that their affectionate loyalty to one another has not evaporated, though it's no longer in any manner expressed. I don't know why I have that feeling so particularly when the visitors are here.

After lunch a procession left the house, slowly crossing the gravel sweep, moving down the avenue. I had not thought to join it, but Mrs Rolleston pressed me. She says quite often, and more these last few busy weeks, that I should not feel tied so to the house. 'Yes, do come,' John James encouraged.

Neither Villana nor Lionel accompanied us, Villana claiming she'd seen the work at the bridge too often, Lionel unable to spare the time. I found myself walking abreast of the Bishop, who at first did not speak and then remembered who I was and wondered if he had been acquainted with my father.

The afternoon was warm and sleepy. When we turned to the left on the road beyond the entrance gates, little puffs of dust rose from each footfall, as dust always does when that surface is dry. I watched it rise and settle, and noted how it was agitated particularly by the heels of Mrs Camier. She walked ahead of the Bishop and myself, her husband on one side of her, her arm in his, Lady Rossboyne on the other. John James was further ahead still, with the Bishop's wife. Villiers Hadnett was on his own, behind us.

'No, I believe I did not,' the Bishop decided. 'I believe I did not have the honour of personal acquaintanceship.'

But word had spread to him of my father's scholarship. The clerical world had long been delighted by my father's thoughts on the Book of Ruth, the Bishop informed me. He coughed and tightly pursed his mouth, as if to punctuate his flow or indicate a change of interest. 'If my memory does not deny me, Sarah, you came up from Bandon to be Villana's governess? Perhaps I take a liberty in saying so, in addressing you as Sarah? None is intended.'

I reassured him. I agreed that his memory was not at fault. I mentioned, since the continuation of the conversation was preferable to silence, the Misses Goodbody's suburban boarding-school, and how subsequently I had spent some years there.

'Oh, dear heavens above, the Misses Goodbody! The good Miss Goodbodys! I knew them well.'

The Bishop in his enthusiasm permitted the sternness that is evident in all the features of his face to slip from most of them at once. It was joyful news, he insisted, that I was not only my father's daughter but also brought memories of two dear ladies. Then the mask deemed suitable for the Bishop of Killaloe returned.

'Sarah, I would not raise this subject with you if we had not come to know one another well in the last few minutes, as indeed I believe we have. Sarah, since I have arrived at Carriglas I have felt troubled. Do you comprehend me?'

I replied cautiously, and the Bishop explained that Mrs

Rolleston had passed on to him her doubt, which he believed he may even have sensed before she spoke.

'Sarah, it would be a most terrible outcome if Villana turned back in church.'

I was saved from the obligation of giving an opinion by Villiers Hadnett catching us up. He launched into speech immediately, informing us that one should endeavour to keep the temperature of one's body constant. Villiers Hadnett is not aware of my dependent position in the household, perhaps even assuming I am another temporary visitor. On the other hand, it is because she does know who I am that Mrs Camier has not addressed me. It is likely that she and I are distantly related: observing me in a rôle akin to a servant's, she would prefer vagueness on that score to remain. So would her husband, who has not yet spoken to me, either. 'I'm thinking of taking a companion-help,' Lady Rossboyne let fall this morning. 'Buttevant's comfier than Carriglas, if ever you thought of it.' I smiled and murmured gratefully.

'I wear an overcoat for that reason,' Villiers Hadnett explained. 'I never travel any distance without an overcoat.'

John James halted and with a gesture of his arm displayed the half-completed bridge. Steel pillars rose strangely from the water, the criss-cross of girders beginning at last to form a pattern. Lady Rossboyne's shrill ejaculation was heard, deploring the spoiling of the landscape. The Bishop pontificated for a moment, discovering God's will in what had come about. The others listened.

John James did not say: 'This will be the bridge of Cornelius Dowley.' Well, naturally he did not. Turning his back upon the workmen and again playfully suggesting that they will not complete their chore, he led the way as we returned to Carriglas, and little puffs of dust again rose from each footfall.

7. Villana's Wedding

Shortly after dawn on the day of the wedding Brigid looked out of the bedroom window of the gate-lodge and said to herself that the weather had held. At Carriglas Patty's alarm clock sounded, and an hour later Mrs Haverty arrived in the kitchen. She asked Brigid if the fish had kept and Brigid replied that it had. The chickens supplied by Mrs Haverty had been stuffed and roasted the day before, and put to cool in the far larder, beside the hams. Before preparing the breakfast dishes Brigid now removed the skin from the hams and dusted them with breadcrumbs. She told Patty to leave the wedding-cake alone. The wedding-cake would remain where it was until the fish and the meats had been eaten. She herself would then arrange for its conveying to the lawn. She repeated all this so that Patty and Mrs Haverty would understand. She reminded them to have kettles boiling for tea when that moment of the day arrived.

The ferryman told Tom that the ferryboat was to be waiting at the pier at ten o'clock and that Mr Coyne would be waiting in one of his motor-cars on the quays to drive everyone to the church. He'd have to make a couple of journeys, and a couple of journeys back. At half-past eleven the ferryboat would be waiting to return the wedding party to the island. It, too, would make as many journeys as were necessary to accommodate the extra guests who'd been in the church. 'I'm invited myself,' the ferryman reminded Tom.

Rows of bottles stood on the stone floor of the near larder: red wine, Tom was told, they contained, and champagne. On the kitchen table the glasses were on trays, which would soon be carried up to the delphinium lawn. 'Did you ever see as much lettuce as that, Tom?' Mrs Haverty remarked in the sculleries, washing the lettuce, leaf by leaf. Near the cold frames in the walled garden he picked mint.

'Just lead her on,' Haverty reminded him later that morning. 'Keep her steady behind me.'

In the governess-car Tom followed the trap which Haverty drove, gripping the reins as he'd been taught. Mr O'Hagan was directly behind him, then came the other traps. Mr O'Hagan was dressed as he might be for Mass or for a funeral, the paleness of his face and his moustache accentuated by the black material of his suit. 'Keep her steady, boy,' Mr O'Hagan said also.

At the pier the horses' heads were held while everyone left the conveyances. Over his navy-blue jersey the ferryman was wearing a navy-blue jacket, which he hadn't been wearing when Tom had talked to him earlier that morning. He held his hand out to receive the passengers, something Tom had never seen him do before.

Tom watched the ferryboat until it reached the other side. Haverty and Mr O'Hagan intended to remain on the pier until the wedding party returned. They sat on the wall and lit cigarettes. They began a discussion about greyhound racing. Tom went back to the house, where he watched his mother chopping the mint on a board at the kitchen table. Then he helped Patty to carry the cutlery to the delphinium lawn. 'I'll show you now, Tom,' she said, and showed him how the knives and forks were laid at each place, with a spoon and a smaller fork.

*

Finnamore changed into the clothes that had been made for him. While he was still eating his breakfast, Eugene Prille had arrived with a rose for his buttonhole. Eugene's small, round cheeks had been affected by a glow of warmth, and Finnamore had received the impression that the day meant almost as much to his clerk as it did to him. Eugene and his wife, who was in every way her husband's twin, would enjoy the outing to Carriglas. They would take a certain pride; Eugene had said as much. Finnamore believed they had cultivated the rose specially.

Items he had read in his newspaper over breakfast had stuck in his mind. A firm of Swedish blanket-manufacturers was seeking representatives to sell its blankets in Ireland. A national government had been formed in England. A meeting of the British Dental Association had taken place in Wales. In Co. Tipperary a man had gone berserk with a pitchfork. A ledger clerk in Arklow had confessed to stealing £15.12s.6d. Lord Fermoy had become engaged.

He believed he would never forget those items of news because he had read them on this day. Nor would he forget the sleepless night he had spent, the doubts that had constantly assailed him, the lingering impression that the Carriglas visitors thought little of him. He would never forget the distressed face of his maid when he had said good morning, nor the way she had smacked down in front of him his two poached eggs. She had not spoken. A week ago he had asked if she intended to stand outside the railings of St Boniface's, as Catholic women often did at Protestant weddings, waiting for the bride. She had curtly replied that she certainly did not.

Having dressed, he clipped his moustache with his nail-scissors. *Why buy new clothes*, an advertisement in the newspaper had asked, *when your garments are only soiled and shiny on the one side?* A woman in Maryborough had kissed a dog and died. It was the day that honoured St Zephyrinus.

*

Seeing the postman pass by, she ran after him, a thing she had never done in her life before. But he only shook his head: that morning he had no letters for the Rose of Tralee.

The family from Dunmanway spoke to her in the hall but she hardly heard them. All day yesterday she hadn't been able to eat a thing, the same again at breakfast. 'You're looking edgy, Mrs Moledy,' McGrath had said to her, and she'd told him to mind his own business before she could stop herself.

A letter could have gone astray, you often heard of it. It could be lying somewhere in the post office, maybe fallen under a shelf. It could have fallen out of a bag. 'God knows,' muttered Mrs Moledy distractedly. 'God alone knows.'

The banknotes were still under the tissue paper, which was a worry also, day after day in a hat-box. Two lines on a piece of paper was all she required, two lines to say he was busy due to the wedding, understandable that he should be. A minute, she had estimated in the night, a single minute of his time, then give it to the ferryman to post. She'd often mentioned that that was how he should do it; she'd gone through the thing with him in case he'd ever catch a cold and she'd be worried.

In her bedroom Mrs Moledy tidied her face, and then felt calmer. He'd understand. He'd see at once that the money wasn't safe in a hat-box, with strangers in the house, and a young maid. She went downstairs again, and opened the door in the hall that led to the basement kitchen. 'I'm going out,' she called down to her maid.

*

Villana entered the church on John James's arm. Respectfully, the congregation rose. Eyes noted the simplicity of the bride's cornflower-blue dress, and the absence of bridesmaids, the modest blue and white sweet-peas she carried. The same eyes followed her progress to the altar, where the two solicitors, bridegroom and best man, were of a height. John James, taller by an inch or so, delivered his sister into the Bishop of Killaloe's care. Beside the Bishop stood Canon Kinchella, white-haired and cherubic, who had baptised the bride in this church twenty-nine years ago. He had not taken it amiss when he'd been told the Bishop had put in a family claim; with the humility that distinguished his long career in the Church of Ireland he had at once agreed to the arrangements that were being made around him.

In the body of the church Mrs Camier stood between her husband and Villiers Hadnett, on whose other side stood the Bishop's wife. Villana was pale, Lady Rossboyne considered, as any girl would be in the circumstances. She wondered if the Pollexfen boy had TB. At Buttevant, six months ago, a wedding had been cancelled because of TB. Generally that was the reason.

In the pews behind these family connections were the wedding guests of the more immediate neighbourhood, women of all ages attired in a variety of colours and a variety of hats, the men sporting here and there a button-hole carnation. The Manserghs were there, and the Fuges, and Sir Cedric Goff, whose suit of plus-fours remained unpaid for. Surgeon Woulfe was there, and Miss de Ryal, and old Zeb Sykes, a clergyman who still did summer duty when a parish sent for him. Mrs Commodium squashed her neighbour into a corner of a pew; the agent at the Bank of Ireland sat more sedately, between his daughter and his wife. There were other people also, the remnants of old families whose genealogy was recorded in the mahogany filing-cabinets of Harbinson and Balt, the children of families that had more lately reached a social height not previously attained.

'And therefore is not by any to be enterprised,' the Bishop of Killaloe reminded his congregation with severity, 'nor taken in hand unadvisedly, lightly or wantonly; but reverently, discreetly, advisedly, soberly, and in the fear of God.'

Mrs Rolleston prayed that even in these final moments something would go wrong. She prayed for a silence, in which her granddaughter would slowly turn her back on the altar and, with her glance fixed on some point in the church, solemnly descend the steps to the aisle, not speaking until she reached the font and lightly rested a hand on it. 'It is only decent to draw back,' she prayed her granddaughter might murmur, quietly, though with a vigour that she believed could not be denied.

There is no reason, John James reflected as he stood there, why there shouldn't be business to do from time to time in Dublin. It would not be difficult to pick up again the family association with Davison's Hotel. The place would have retained its modest style; there was a cosiness, he recalled, about the polished hall; the waitresses in the small dining-room were pleasantly uniformed. You could sit for hours in the privacy of the smoking-room, with a whiskey and soda or chatting to a friend. There was no reason why he shouldn't move the bank account to a city branch on the grounds that it would be better looked after by city clerks. The clothes sold in Lett's Arcade left a bit to be desired. His leg might need to be examined from time to time by someone more expert on legs than a provincial doctor. While the Bishop's voice continued, John James strolled down a Dublin street and then politely called out because a pretty woman in black had dropped a glove.

'For be ye well assured, that so many as are coupled together otherwise than God's Word doth allow are not joined together by God; neither is their Matrimony lawful.'

Lionel tried to listen, but he kept seeing his sister running about the garden, she and he hiding while John James and Hugh counted to a hundred. In some bedroom on the way to Killarney Finnamore Balt would embrace her with lips that were like leather dried in the sun. The uncomfortable-looking moustache above them would roughen her cheeks; in her presence he would take the shoes from his feet. For a moment Lionel wished he had spoken, as once he would have, pleading with her and cajoling. But Villana, of course, would not have listened.

'Wilt thou have this Woman,' the Bishop enquired of Finnamore, 'to thy wedded wife, to live together after God's ordinance in the holy estate of Matrimony? Wilt thou love her, comfort her, honour and keep her, in sickness and in health; and forsaking all others, keep thee only unto her, so long as ye both shall live?'

A child whispered and was hushed. 'Fortunate I was behind you,' John James remarked to the woman in black. 'Another few paces and it would be gone for ever.' He dusted the glove before returning it to her, and when the woman thanked him and turned into a teashop he allowed a few minutes to go by before turning into it also. 'Do you terribly mind?' he said through a smile. 'I'm afraid there isn't an empty table.'

'Wilt thou have this Man,' the Bishop enquired of Villana, 'to thy wedded husband, to live together after God's ordinance in the holy estate of Matrimony? Wilt thou obey him, and serve him, love, honour and keep him, in sickness and in health; and forsaking all others, keep thee only unto him, so long as ye both shall live?'

Mrs Rolleston leaned forward. Again she prayed that her granddaughter would draw back. But because there was no immediate response to his question the Bishop pleaded also, that he should not be made a fool of. For a few more moments the clash of these desires hung unresolved above the wedding guests, before the Bishop was rewarded.

'I will,' Villana promised.

*

After she'd had three glasses of whiskey and hot water in Myley Flynn's Mrs Moledy felt better. She walked down to

Coyne's Garage to make sure the French motor-car was still on the premises. 'I'm after driving them up to the church in it,' Mr Coyne said. 'To see if they'd like the feel of it.' She called in to Myley Flynn's on the way back to the boarding-house, not taking long about it because the last thing she wanted was to find herself involved with boatloads of Protestants on their way over to the wedding breakfast. What would suit her was to cross over herself while they were still in the church and then be quietly waiting for him somewhere in his gardens, not noticeable because of the crowds. She'd never have thought of doing it if she hadn't had the few drinks in, she'd never have had the neck for it. In her bedroom she changed into the claret and cream outfit she'd bought in Lett's a year ago. She transferred the money she'd got for him from the hat-box to her handbag.

'That's a walk and a half,' she said, arriving some time later on a lawn with flowers all around it, where a boy and a young maid were laying knives and forks on a table. The pair of them gawked at her, just like the old ferryman had when she'd stepped on to his boat, just like O'Hagan from the post office had when she'd stepped off it. She couldn't understand what O'Hagan was doing there, sitting on a wall beside a dog-cart. She asked the other man to give her a lift up to the house, but he said he couldn't unless she waited until after the guests had come across. So she'd had to walk, which hadn't been easy in the shoes she was wearing.

'Have you a Power's for me?' she suggested to the young one and the boy, but they only went on gawking at her, so she sat down at one end of the table with the cutlery on it. The sister would probably be placed there, with Balt down the other end. The sister wasn't right in the head, getting tied up to the like of Balt.

'I'll go in and ask my mother,' the boy said, and she recognised him from seeing him at Mass. He was the misfortune that had resulted after one of the maids got herself up the pole.

'What's your name?' she asked the young one, who'd begun to put out the forks again.

'Patty, ma'am.'

'D'you know who I am, Patty? Did you recognise me when you saw me?'

'You're Mrs Moledy from the boarding-house.'

'Did you ever hear me mentioned in the kitchen, Patty? What type of thing would they say?'

'I never heard you mentioned, Mrs Moledy.'

She eyed the girl doubtfully. Full of lies they were mostly. She'd said it to him only a week ago, but he'd shown no sympathy. She'd told him about a lie concerning fly-papers, told to her in her own kitchen. But when she'd looked at him again he was asleep.

'Good morning to you, Mrs Moledy.' The boy had returned with his mother, who looked flustered, with her sleeves rolled up. She was wearing a blue overall, not as smartly turned out as the young one in the uniform. These were the two trollops he'd said he might as well be married to when she'd made the suggestion to him. Ridiculous talk that was, a man of his years. 'Were you looking for someone?' the one who'd got herself up the pole was asking, as bold as brass.

She laughed, considering a laugh the best answer to give to a serving woman who was standing in the company of her disgrace. The woman asked the question again, and she replied that she was looking for a drink on account of having time to put in.

'There's no Power's in the house. Only Jameson or Paddy.'

'What's wrong with a Paddy?'

The woman went away, and returned with such a modest quantity of whiskey in a glass that Mrs Moledy had to laugh again, not that she drank much as a rule. 'I want you in the kitchen,' the woman told the young one, and told the boy to look out the top landing window and see if the ferry was coming with the visitors. She told him not to be late down at the pier. Then all three of them disappeared.

Mrs Moledy took a mouthful of whiskey, wishing there was hot water to go with it, but you couldn't expect everything. You had to be fair about a thing like that, but even so she saw no harm in resting herself, the condition her feet were in. She'd slip away into the trees long before the crowd arrived. She'd call out to him softly and give him the notes, explaining that she was worried because of the strangers in the house. She would explain to him that you couldn't leave a thimble about these days. Better to be safe than sorry, she'd say, and after that she wouldn't delay him. 'I hear Coyne drove to the church in the car,' she'd say, only that and nothing else.

It was pleasant in the sunshine. Bees were humming near to where she sat. The flowers that were all around her gave off a heady fragrance. Pleasurably, she savoured another mouthful of whiskey. He'd never seen her claret before and she wondered what he'd think of it, not that he ever remarked on clothing. She remembered telling him about it at the time, and how she'd had to stand on the counter after the shop was closed while Mrs Lett and Lett got the hem right. She'd wanted to take it out of the wardrobe and put it on for him but she never had.

Noticing that her glass had become empty, Mrs Moledy rose and made her way into the house through the open French windows. 'There's nothing can't be put right with a drop of Paddy,' was a favourite axiom of the big trawler-man who came into Myley Flynn's, a fresh-faced man with exploded veins all over his nose and cheeks. In her own view Power's was the better drink, but what wasn't there you couldn't have. She found the bottle of Paddy among the sherry decanters on the sideboard.

Afterwards Mrs Moledy recalled making several journeys to the sideboard. She recalled saying to herself how partylike the flowers were, and how the long table looked lovely with its clean white tablecloths. Three old sheepdogs came and slumped down beside her, as tame and friendly as you could ask for. 'Isn't it nice here?' she said whenever the young one appeared with something else for the table, but the only response she received was a giggle.

In time other people appeared. His brother peered out of the dining-room, dressed up in fancy togs. A female with forget-me-nots on her dress came out and spoke to her. She thought it was the sister so she held out her hand, even though she was puzzled by the reduced size of her and wondered if she'd suffered an attack of something.

'I'm Noreen Moledy,' she said. 'We never met.'

But she realised while she was speaking that this wasn't the sister at all. This was a serious-faced little creature, not smiling like a bride would be. 'Haven't I seen you in the shops?' she said, and some kind of reply was made, only the poor creature's voice was so low no one could have heard it. In an effort at friendliness, she patted the chair beside her, remarking how pleasant it was, with the smell of the flowers and the dogs fast asleep. Then she remembered that this was the female who'd been hanging about the place for years, some type of poor relation. She closed her eyes in order to rest them, resolving to give herself another five minutes before she slipped away into the trees. When she opened them she found herself alone, which she considered rude because she'd been thinking of something to say that would interest the female with the forget-me-nots on her clothing. She had it on the tip of her tongue to tell her about the altering of the hem, only you couldn't talk to someone who wasn't there so she made her way to the dining-room. She approached the sideboard, once more recalling the trawler-man who came into Myley Flynn's. She filled her glass to the brim.

'She must have gone,' the old grandmother was saying when she returned to the lawn, a woman she knew well by sight. 'Thank God for that.'

Mrs Moledy sat down on a chair and carefully placed her glass on the table. The female had gone all right, she said; one minute she was there and the next she'd walked off. She closed one eye because all of a sudden there appeared to be two of the old grandmothers in front of her. She wondered if the other female was suffering from toothache, which would account for being so serious in the face. She asked about that, but although she could see the women's lips moving, she couldn't hear what they said. She couldn't understand why none of these people would speak up, and then she wondered if they were able to hear what she was saying herself.

'Excuse me, were we ever introduced? Noreen Moledy, originally of Cahir.'

She held out her hand in the direction of the two women, but by mistake she closed her eyes for a minute and the next thing was they weren't there any more. She felt tired so she went to sleep.

*

The governess-car and the dog-cart and the traps journeyed repeatedly between the pier and the house. 'If I may assist,' Eugene Prille offered, and John James was relieved of his trap. Mr O'Hagan succeeded in making his horse trot. Haverty shook the reins to make his hurry up. Tom didn't dare do that.

Eugene Prille resembled an egg, Deso Furphy had once said. Mrs Prille, whom Tom had only occasionally seen before, resembled an egg also. 'Don't leave me,' he heard her begging her husband when he made his offer, and seemed happy to accompany him back and forth in the trap, both of them smiling all the time.

'You were not made a fool of,' the Bishop's wife observed as Tom turned the governess-car into the avenue.

'A bishop should not be,' came the retort, pointed with asperity. 'That was all I ever meant.'

No further exchange took place between them, but on the next journey Villiers Hadnett, at very great length, recalled for Miss de Ryal and old Zeb Sykes the wedding of his sister. The ceremony had been interrupted by an objector, a young man who had been a suitor of Villiers Hadnett's sister in the past. This youth had shouted out from the back of the church, announcing that he intended to burn it down unless matters were halted.

'Dear me.' Miss de Ryal, who had once given Tom a penny she'd found on the street, was all in white, her reddened lips standing out because her face was white also. She was older than she looked, Mrs Haverty had been saying to Tom's mother only the other morning.

'He was seized hold of by the arms,' Villiers Hadnett went on. 'He had matches secreted all over him and two tins of petrol in the vestry.'

'How horrid for your sister!'

'My sister is injudicious.'

'In all my years in the Church of Ireland,' old Zeb Sykes contributed, 'I did not have an experience like that.'

Tom listened while the further details of the events were recounted, the seizing of the ex-suitor, the removal of boxes of matches from his pockets, his subsequent escape from custody in the vestry, the second interruption of the ceremony, the discovery of more petrol and matches.

'How very dreadful!' politely murmured Miss de Ryal, but Villiers Hadnett, warmly wrapped in his overcoat and muffler, had already changed the subject and was telling his companions about the expense and discomfort of his journey from Athlone. 'I don't know if you're aware,' he said, 'that especially when travelling the body temperature must be constant.'

Some of the guests began to walk from the pier and hailed Tom as he came towards them on his way back from the house. Haverty had showed him how to turn the pony round, which he managed to do if he took it slowly. 'Can you hurry up a bit?' a woman urged on the avenue, but Haverty had told him he mustn't so he pretended not to understand her.

When all the wedding guests had been delivered, the traps and the governess-car and the dog-cart stood in the yard, waiting until they were again required. 'You're offered a glass of sherry,' Haverty informed Mr O'Hagan, adding that when the time came there'd be a place for him at the kitchen table. He'd try the sherry, Mr O'Hagan cautiously assented.

Tom watched the party from the side of the house, where he couldn't be seen. People stood with glasses in their hands beneath the strawberry trees, or strolled out of sight round the corner of the conservatory. Their laughter and their raised voices carried to where he watched. Children who were older than he was stood obediently by their parents, younger ones ran about on the grass. Two men came out of the house and crossed the gravel, both of them smoking cigarettes, with glasses in their hands. 'It'd be ripe if he turned out not to have a fluke,' one of them said, and the other laughed.

When everyone sat down at the table on the delphinium lawn Tom's task would be to go all over the garden in search of any glasses that had been put down. He was to carry them to the kitchen, two at a time, not running in case he tripped. Patty wouldn't have time to do that, nor would Mrs Haverty. There would be no one to help him, and the glasses would have to be collected so that they could be washed in case there was a shortage afterwards. Later on it would be the same with the teacups.

'Fish,' the man who had forgotten to give him the threepenny-piece said to the woman who had reminded him that he should. 'And a couple of seedy-looking chickens.'

Speculating on the quality of the hams that accompanied the chickens, the Camiers passed as close to Tom as the two men with the cigarettes had. In the greater distance he watched Mrs Rolleston moving among her guests, shaking their hands and pausing to talk to them. Some of them he had never seen before.

He went all the way round the house until the people standing beneath the strawberry trees came into view again. Mrs Rolleston was still going from one person to another. Cautiously he moved closer, making his way through the shrubbery that skirted one side of the grass. Towering rhododendron bushes and bamboos kept him concealed. He gazed through foliage at silk dresses and dark suits. The laughter and voices had become louder. Villiers Hadnett was telling Miss de Ryal about his lung.

'She keeps a boarding-house,' another voice said, but Tom was unable to ascertain who was speaking because he couldn't see around a clump of bamboo canes. It might be Mrs Commodium, he thought, because the voice was what you'd expect from her: gruff and heavy. Mrs Commodium was a statuesque woman who moved very slowly down South Main Street, calling in at the shops and ordering goods to be sent to her house. Once, in Meath's, Tom had heard two other women agreeing that she had driven her husband to his grave. Tom remembered seeing Mr Commodium in his lifetime, a man with a dog on a lead.

'But what on earth is she doing here?' someone else enquired, sounding like the woman who'd asked him to show her the place his father had been killed.

'He visits her, you know. You could set your clocks by him.' Tom heard a gasp, and an effort at speech failing, another effort made and again failing. 'Oh, indeed he does,' the voice he guessed to be Mrs Commodium's insisted. 'Everyone knows that.'

The conversation drifted away from Tom, the voices unintelligibly continuing for a moment longer. He slipped through the shrubbery, making his way to another edge of it. 'Tom!' he heard Mrs Rolleston calling, and then he saw her on the delphinium lawn. 'Patty, tell Tom I want him,' she said as Patty went by with a jug of lemonade he had watched being made in the kitchen.

He ran out on to the short grass of the lawn, pursuing Mrs Rolleston, who had passed into the house. In the dining-room he said:

'I'm here, Mrs Rolleston.'

Apart from the sculleries and the kitchen, his mother didn't allow him to go into any room of the house unless he was sent on a message, but he knew it was all right to be in the dining-room because Mrs Rolleston wanted him. She didn't hear him at first so he repeated her name more loudly. She turned round just as she was about to pass through the door to the inner hall.

'Tom, would you do something for me?'

She paused the way she did when she asked him to buy a postal order, not taking it for granted that he'd agree before he said so. He liked her the best of them, Tom thought.

'I will, Mrs Rolleston,' he said.

'Tom, after lunch, will you show the children places to hide? Make them play a game of hide-and-seek.'

He nodded, although he felt shy at the thought of approaching the children.

'And make sure you get your own lunch in the kitchen, Tom.'

She passed into the inner hall and Tom left the dining-room by the French windows. Mrs Moledy was still sitting on her own at the long table; other people were standing near it. He skirted the lawn, then re-entered the shrubbery to continue his observation. The Bishop was talking while his wife and another woman listened. Old Zeb Sykes was sitting down on the grass and children were playing some kind of game around him, decorating him with daisy chains. Eugene Prille and his wife were arm in arm.

*

'I need to get into the trees,' Mrs Moledy said to the Bishop of Killaloe. 'I shouldn't be loitering here.'

'Trees?'

'I'm here on business, as a matter of fact.'

The glass she'd filled to the brim was still on the table in front of her. She lifted it to her lips and found that the whiskey it contained had been pleasantly warmed by the sun. She remarked upon this to the Bishop, adding that she always preferred the addition of a drop of warm water, although she hadn't asked for it, not being in a public house. 'Haven't they a lovely place here, though?' she said, endeavouring to be friendly.

Other people were beginning to sit down. She waved at a man from the Bank of Ireland, whom she knew to talk to, and at Miss de Ryal, whom she knew by sight. The Commodium female was there, extraordinary that they'd invite the like of that.

'Well, isn't this great?' she remarked to the Bishop.

'Isn't what great?'

'Errah, go on with you!' She nudged his elbow with her own. As soon as she'd finished the contents of her glass she'd slip away, no trouble to anyone. At the far end of the table, where the old grandmother was being assisted on to a chair, the sister was directing people to other chairs. He was standing just behind her, directing people also. She waved at him when he was looking straight at her, but he took no notice.

Someone sat down on her other side, a young fellow with glasses. She gave a laugh because he was wearing an overcoat on a day that would bake the bones in your back. She asked him about it and he said that everyone should put an overcoat on before sitting down outside.

'Errah, go on with you!' She nudged him also. 'Don't be codding me,' she said, and then forgot about him because for an unpleasant moment she thought she'd lost her bag with the money in it. She felt for it at her feet and to her relief found that it was safely there. She opened it and counted the notes. 'I have money for a motor-car,' she explained to the clergyman. 'I'm not due at the breakfast, to tell you the truth. Only there's business to be fixed.' She tried to explain the same thing to the young fellow in the overcoat, but he was slow on the uptake so she left it.

'Motor-car?' the clergyman said.

'There's a French car that Coyne has. D'you know Coyne at all?'

She described the garage man in case the clergyman would have seen him on the streets – the rosary-bead eyes and the way his head shone, and his paunchiness. He kept the little strands of his moustache tidy with hair oil, she said. He had a wife and eleven daughters.

'I'm in no way acquainted with this man,' the clergyman said, and she agreed that he probably wouldn't be. She explained that the car they'd come from the church in was the vehicle in question. According to Coyne, there wasn't one to touch it on the roads of Ireland. According to what he'd said to her, you couldn't beat the Frenchman when it came to building a motor-car. The Frenchman reigned supreme in the motor-car department.

'I see,' was the reply she received, without an accompanying smile.

'Balt has a Ford. You see it in the streets. IF 92.'

'I know nothing about motor-cars.'

The notes were all present, still held by the rubber-band Corcoran in the Munster and Leinster had put around them. She thought about asking the man if he knew Corcoran at all, but she changed her mind and asked him his name instead.

'I'm the Bishop of Killaloe.'

'Well, glory be to God!'

The maid placed a plate of food in front of her, not that she was hungry. Down at the end of the table he was carving a fish, and the brother was cutting at a ham and a couple of chickens. The brother was good-looking in his way. No doubt about it, all three of them had looks.

'Just a slice of chicken breast,' the fellow in the overcoat said, handing back his plate of fish.

'I'm Noreen Moledy,' she said. 'I married into a house in the town.'

The young fellow didn't acknowledge that, but you could see he was worried about all these plates of food, the last thing anyone wanted on a hot day like this. 'What's your name?' she said to him, and he told her but she couldn't catch it. He had been staying with an uncle near Athlone, he said; he'd had a terrible journey down through the country in order to attend the wedding. He was considered delicate, he told her as well.

'You have a delicate look to you all right.'

The brother began to go round with a bottle of champagne. Other bottles had been brought out from the house and were standing on the grass at the edge of the flowerbed. 'Or would you prefer a glass of burgundy?' the brother said when he came to her, as nice as anything.

'Ah no, no, I must definitely be going.' She'd have stood up only she was afraid of feeling groggy due to the sun. 'I was drinking Paddy,' she explained to the brother. 'There's some inside there on the sideboard.'

She waved down the table again, smiling at everyone in case they hadn't noticed the little movement of her hand. If he looked up from carving the fish she'd point at the bag, which she'd put on the table in front of her for safety. As soon as she caught his eye she'd get up on to her feet, groggy or not, so that he could see where she was heading and come on after her. Funny the Prille fellow being invited, and the wife with him.

'I'm a widow myself,' she said to the Bishop, feeling he should know that before they went any further. She told him about the death that had taken place in a back bedroom of the Rose of Tralee, how it had had to be a

bedroom at the back owing to the boarding-house proprietor's aversion to sunlight.

'I said to Woulfe would he operate but you could be
talking to the wall.' She waved across the table at the
medical man in question to show that no offence had been
taken, then she took the ten-pound notes out of her
handbag and counted them again. 'D'you know Corcoran
in the Munster and Leinster?' she said.

The Bishop replied that he was not of the neighbourhood. He was not acquainted with the local people. He had
noticed the man who'd driven the motor-car to and from
the church, but he could not claim that he had in any way
got to know him. He hadn't even spoken to him.

'That's Coyne you're talking about. Corcoran's a different kettle of fish.'

'I am not acquainted with Mr Corcoran either.'

'Are you acquainted with McGrath? Or Tobin?'

'I'm afraid not.'

She explained to him who they were, quiet and decent the
two of them. 'The foreman out at the bridge is a fellow by
the name of Ernie Cassidy.'

'Look, I really don't know any of these people.'

'Errah, why would you? Isn't it great about the bridge,
though? I was saying the other day they won't know
themselves.'

'The bridge is the wrong side of the island for Carriglas, it
seems.'

'They've a right to complain about that. Like they have
about Corny Dowley's name going up on it.'

'I doubt very much that the Rollestons would make
complaints.'

'Wouldn't Balt do it for them, though? Didn't he send a
letter to the county council about the Dowley thing?'

'I'm afraid I don't follow you.'

She wondered if the man was affected in the brain. She
watched him eating his fish, the fork going up and down,

the single face becoming two and then one of the faces sliding away altogether. It was Dowley who killed the butler, she explained in case the man was ignorant. You couldn't blame Balt for raising the roof over the bridge business.

He looked at her with his mouth open. He was another of them who was slow on the uptake, which you wouldn't expect in a bishop of his church. He was slow the way he'd mixed up Corcoran and Coyne, thinking it was Corcoran's car he'd been given a lift in when it was a known fact that Corcoran didn't even possess a bicycle.

'You wouldn't have been acquainted with Dowley,' she said in case he got into another muddle over that. She didn't want to continue looking at him because of the way his face was behaving, so she turned her head away. Unfortunately the faces of the wedding guests who were nearest to her became confused in much the same manner. The paleness of Miss de Ryal was suddenly cheered by a florid tinge from her neighbour. The fleshy neck of the Bishop's wife shifted to the right and ended by dressing the gaunt bones of Surgeon Woulfe, whose own hooked nose was borrowed by Mrs Prille. The unadorned countenance of Sir Cedric Goff acquired the make-up of Mrs Camier, the moustache of the bridegroom crept towards the faded features of Lady Rossboyne. Old Zeb Sykes developed a lopsided look, children aged. Protestants to a man, she said to herself, or said it aloud, she wasn't sure which. Protestants and none the worse for it: you knew where you were with Protestants.

'Tell him I'll be in the trees,' she said to the brother when he came by the next time with his wine bottles. 'Tell him to give a whistle.' But when she began to get up she again decided it was foolish to attempt to do so.

*

Tom couldn't bring himself to approach the children, but it didn't matter because they had thought of playing hide-and-seek themselves. In the left-hand scullery Mrs Haverty and his mother washed the dishes. The ferryman had arrived in the kitchen, and Mr O'Hagan was there, and Haverty. There were glasses on the table, and a bottle that hadn't been opened yet.

When the lunch came to an end Tom was allowed to help Patty to carry the food that remained in from the lawn. Fragments of conversation continued to reach him, several of the people talking about Mrs Moledy counting her money. In the kitchen his mother and Mrs Haverty said it was shocking, and Patty said it was shocking also. A child had spilt a glass of lemonade on the tablecloth, Patty said, and the child's mother had made a fuss, but no one had upbraided Mrs Moledy, and nobody woke her up when she kept falling asleep. She'd applauded loudly when the wedding-cake was cut, but everyone had been very polite about it.

'I shouldn't have let her sit there in the first place,' Tom's mother said, but a few minutes later the bride arrived in the kitchen and the episode appeared to be forgotten. Mr Balt arrived in the kitchen also, standing by the door at first, but then coming further in and proceeding to open the bottle on the table.

'Are there glasses?' he said.

The ferryman and Mr O'Hagan and Haverty were on their feet, their cigarettes cupped in hands held behind their backs. There were glasses for everyone, Patty included, but Tom wasn't noticed until slices of the wedding-cake were passed round and Mrs Haverty pushed him forward.

'Good health to you both.' The ferryman took the lead, raising his glass in the air, higher than anyone in the garden had raised a glass. 'Good luck and good health,' the ferryman said. The others raised their glasses also, and Tom looked from the glasses to the married couple, who had linked arms with one another. It didn't occur to him that Mr Balt was too old for her, although he could see he was the older of the two. It wasn't until some years later that he noticed the oddity of it.

*

Motoring westward in Finnamore's motor-car, the married couple did not speak much. Villana endeavoured to sleep, the late afternoon sun warm on her face. Finnamore drove steadily, at thirty-five miles an hour, engrossed in his thoughts. He had often heard of John James's friendship with the woman from the boarding-house, but as a matter of legal principle had always denied its truth. The counting of the banknotes, the rubber-band temporarily between the woman's lips: for a long time, Finnamore speculated, that image would haunt his consciousness.

'A pity.'

'Oh, none of it matters.'

Villana lit a cigarette and within a few moments the confined interior of the car filled with tobacco smoke. Finnamore was about to mention the woman's waving at people, but desisted in case he should seem to be complaining overmuch. Instead he said:

'We are alone at last.'

Villana closed her eyes again. When she felt the ash of her cigarette warm between her fingers she wound down the window and flicked the cork-tipped inch that remained on to the road. They were to spend this night in Cork, the journey all the way to the Killarney lakes being too long an afternoon's drive: the Imperial Hotel had been recommended by her husband's partner as being particularly comfortable. She was glad the ferryman had come to the kitchen and that Haverty's friend, Mr O'Hagan, had been there. It was good of both of them to have helped in the way they had.

'Yes,' she said. 'We are alone.'

Miss de Ryal had played the piano in the drawing-room. Quite suddenly there had been the music drifting faintly to the garden, a piece by Schubert, who was the only composer Miss de Ryal ever played. Villana was glad, too, that someone had urged Miss de Ryal to sit down on the old, embroidered piano-stool, as so often she had done in the past. It made things agreeable again after the incident with John James's woman. There'd been clapping in the drawing-room when a piece came to an end.

A man wheeling a bicycle saluted them. They passed through a village. A woman waved, driving a cow across the road, in through an open gate.

'I certainly don't intend to stagnate my days away at Carriglas,' John James used to say as a boy. And although Lionel had put it differently he, too, had been determined to escape the easy nostalgia of childhood. She herself had never had such feelings.

The car drew in at the hotel Harbinson had recommended. Suitcases were carried to a bedroom, and unpacked. In a drab dining-room they ate the dinner that had been prepared for them.

'It is an extremely long time,' Villana said, pushing her knife and fork together, 'since I spent a night away from Carriglas.'

'You would have been a little girl.'

He saw her then: in one red dress or another, her plaits of corn-coloured hair, impudence in her eyes when she climbed on to his knees to play with his watch and its chain.

'Yes, I would have been a little girl.'

Hours later in the darkness, while he slept beside her, Villana caused the day that had passed to pass again. In the long looking-glass of her bedroom at Carriglas the corn-flower blue of her wedding-dress was a pale reflection of her eyes. Beneath the hem that almost reached the floor her bare toes protruded. These were her last moments alone, she had thought, sitting on the edge of her bed, the skirt of her dress pulled up just a little in order to cross her legs. She'd lit a Craven A.

'Dear child,' he whispered in his sleep. 'My darling girl.'

Would this make a difference, she wondered, or whenever she entered the ice-house would she still feel the past clinging like lichen to its walls? Hugh's love had remained at Carriglas like the ghost of a person; it had begun there and been laid to rest there. 'It is impossible,' he had adamantly laid down, his firmness of purpose making the sacrifice he insisted upon seem heroic and even beautiful. While they still embraced, the act of destruction had been committed.

All day, ridiculously, she had believed he might suddenly be there. All day she had believed that she would wake to find herself walking out of a nightmare that had lasted for only a few seconds. But all there'd been was the occasion she had brought upon herself – wedding guests celebrating a marriage that was a local wonder, her brother's woman drunk. Tomorrow they would continue their journey and then they would walk by the lakes. The affection that cheered her in her desolation would not have departed from her husband's eyes; reflected in every tone of his voice, in all his glances and his gestures, it would continue to soothe her pain. When the moment was suitable she would gently tell him that it was better to let Carriglas go, that his dream of resurrection was not what anyone wanted. He would be disappointed and bewildered, as he had been when she'd explained about the dedication on the bridge. But in the end he would accept the family's wishes and abide by them.

*

John James refused the incident entry to his mind. He forced his thoughts away from it, bludgeoning them recklessly, tolerating no disobedience. At least he had remembered the carpentry man's name; at least there was that minuscule mercy. Asquith-Jones had protested that it was common assault to strike anyone with a panel saw, and

Spokeshave Billimore had called him a pup, and Asquith-Jones had said he wouldn't take that from a carpentry instructor. Asquith-Jones had kept a caged rat in his dormitory locker, a tawny-coloured creature that would gnaw the end of your fingers if you put them between the bars. Someone else – Grub Hineforth it would have been – let it out once.

Tomorrow they would go. The last trapful of them would be on its way down the avenue by half-past ten. He doubted very much that he'd ever lay eyes on Villiers Hadnett or the Camiers, or any of them, again. 'There's not a man can hold a candle to you': the slur of her voice slipped through his lines of defence, her hand on his arm, her body teetering on the heels of her shoes, the banknotes yet again taken from the handbag. Grub Hineforth had gone down at Passchendaele too. He tried to remember his face. Was it he or Barmy Jessop who'd had a peculiar nose? 'My soldier boy,' she'd whispered, telling him she was keeping her voice down because she knew it was what he wanted. He'd had to take the money because she'd never have gone. He'd bundled it into a pocket and turned his back on her.

Again he steadied his thoughts, dragging any protection he could into his mind. 'No, no, I insist.' He paid for their tea and then they sauntered on the street since the afternoon was mild. He was staying in Davison's Hotel, he said; he always stayed there, a family thing really. She had a pretty smile, and grey eyes that were a little nervous. In the teashop, when she'd taken her coat off, there'd been a tiny brooch, a single sapphire in a gold setting, pinned to the black material of her dress. A hat you hardly noticed – black also – was worn a little to one side. 'I've often gone by Davison's,' she said. 'Awfully nice, it seems.' He told her how he'd stayed there with his brother, on the way back and forth to school in England, how his father had hired one of Davison's waiters to become the last of their butlers. 'We might dine together one evening?' he suggested, and when they did so he told her about the worst day of his life, the day his sister had married an elderly solicitor and how an uninvited guest had become drunk in a way that seemed typical of life as it was nowadays. 'How horrid for you,' his companion murmured. 'How horridly distressing.'

*

Carriglas, August 26th, 1931. I remained in the drawing-room, alone, when it was late. The tweed of the jacket I repaired was brown with flecks of grey in it, harsh between my fingers, a smell of the farmyard still adhering to it. Its pockets had been pulled out of shape, two buttons missing, a seam undone at the shoulders. My lips dampened the thread in preparation for the needle's eye, and then the needle slipped away beneath the pressure of my thimble, the grey thread drawing back and forth. For a moment I seemed to hear again Miss de Ryal's Schubert pieces although Miss de Ryal had been gone for hours. 'What a day it's been, Sarah!' he said an hour ago, and for a moment I thought he was going to say something else, but he did not.

8. Carriglas in Autumn

There was an accident at the bridge. A steel girder, being passed into place, escaped the grasp of two of the men who hoisted it, and fell heavily upon a third man, trapping him beneath it. When the weight was lifted from him the man was found to have injuries to the shoulder and a thigh, later diagnosed as shattered bones. Work was suspended while his companions awaited the arrival of a doctor, who ordered the construction of a stretcher and the removal of the injured man from the site. The foreman had known accidents before; a bridge was rarely built without one. He drove the lorry in the back of which three men held the stretcher steady, raised between wooden blocks. Half a day's work was lost but when, that same afternoon, the engineer who had designed the bridge stood discussing its progress with the county council surveyor, they nodded over the half-completed construction, well pleased with the progress that had been made. They walked together to the foreman's shed and consulted him. By December – before Christmas, or at least by the end of the year – there would be traffic on the bridge, he guaranteed. Ever since the work had begun he'd said so, whenever he felt a promise was expected of him.

That same day Tom walked in South Main Street with Neck Daly and Deso Furphy, listening to Deso Furphy's stories about his crazed aunt in Kanturk. Neck Daly went into Barry's and asked Mrs Barry for a liquorice pipe on tick and Mrs Barry told him to go away before she called the Guards. Most of the other shops were closed because it was the half day. Deso Furphy and Neck Daly were on their way to the promenade to annoy people by throwing pebbles at them from behind the old billiard-hall. If they were caught the Brothers would give them the strap, they said. They were nonchalant, showing off a bit, but once Tom had seen Brother Crotty cuffing Deso Furphy outside the picture house because he'd been annoying Humpy Geehan, and Deso Furphy had cried. 'Be seeing you,' they said, one after the other, in the same nonchalant way, and Tom turned into Narrow Lane and went down to the quays. He had to wait for an hour before the ferryboat set off, the ferryman being delayed in the turf accountant's, and then in Spillane's.

On the island Tom left his schoolbag in the gate-lodge and took the path to the holy well, since he had nothing else to do before his mother came down from the house. Not far from the abbey ruins he heard voices.

'God, you'd torment a man!' Briscoe, the bank porter, was there with the girl from Renehan's who'd told Tom she said prayers for him. They were lying on the grass by one of the tumbled-down walls, Briscoe with his jacket off. The girl had her arms around his neck, but now and again she pushed at him, telling him to get off. Tom stood where he was, staring at them. The bank porter's striped brown jacket was lying on the grass. One of his hands had pulled her skirt up. 'Stop that now,' she said, but he took no notice. He pushed her further back on the grass, and Tom could see his face coming down close to hers and his mouth kissing her. All the time he was continuing to pull at her skirt and she was trying to stop him, even though she had one arm round his neck. As Tom watched, her underclothes were exposed, and then the flesh of her thighs. 'Ah, go easy now, for God's sake!' she cried out.

Tom gasped. He wished Neck Daly and Deso Furphy had

come over to the island so that they could see. The girl's stockings were hanging down her legs, and Briscoe was clumsily undoing the buttons of her blouse, kneeling on her arms so that she couldn't resist him. 'God, you have the fine legs,' he said, his voice thickly slurred, like Drunk Paddy's when he was shouting at the seagulls. 'God, you're great!'

'Will you leave me alone? Will you get up and behave yourself?' She said something else but again Tom couldn't hear what it was. The porter told her to have sense. 'D'you love me?' the girl said.

'Amn't I telling you? You're great altogether.'

'You said you loved me the other night.'

The porter's face bent into hers again. He moved his knees so that she could put her arms around his neck. He murmured and she murmured back, and then suddenly he stood up and shouted at her.

'That's the end of it so. That's the finish of the whole caboodle as far as I'm concerned.'

She covered herself. She sat up on the grass, buttoning her blouse. Neither of them noticed Tom standing there although if they'd looked they would have seen him straight away.

'You're a right bitch,' Briscoe shouted at the girl.

Tom gasped again. He could feel a hotness at the back of his neck, creeping round into his cheeks. As quietly as he could, he went away, his eyes still wide.

'A right little convent whore!' Briscoe's voice shouted, and in the same rough voice he swore at the girl, calling her names Tom thought only the boys at the Christian Brothers' used. Crossing an expanse of heather to the cliffs, he walked along the cliff edge, now and again looking down at the waves breaking over the black rocks far below. A piteous note had come into the girl's voice when she'd asked the porter if he loved her. She'd whimpered when he'd abused her.

Tom knew it was what Holy Mullihan meant, with all his

talk about sinning. Once he'd gone with Neck Daly and Deso Furphy to the goat field behind the corn yard and they'd waited for one of the goats to climb up on another. Neck Daly said there wasn't an animal that existed that didn't do that. 'Even two rats,' he'd said. The older boys had eyed Tom closely to see what his reactions would be, and he'd guessed that was the only reason they'd brought him with them. It was how he'd come to be born himself, he'd thought afterwards, his mother and father in a field somewhere because they weren't married. 'That's filthy dirty, Tom,' Holy Mullihan had said when he'd found out about watching the goats. Holy Mullihan found out about everything; he had eyes in the back of his head. 'Don't ever do that again, Tom. Give me a promise now.' Neck Daly and Deso Furphy would have told him to take a running jump at himself, but Tom promised because it was easier.

He walked inland again, on a road that was flat and straight, with turf bogs on either side of it. His mother would have lain there like the fish-sheds girl, protesting and yet putting her arms round the man. 'There'd be people who'd think that, all right,' Holy Mullihan had said. 'About how a sin would definitely contaminate them.'

On the road a shawled woman in a donkey and butt caught up with him. The woman slowed the pace of the donkey so that she could talk to him. He'd seen the donkey tied up at the pier. She'd been over to get meal for her fowls, the woman said; she lived near where the bridge was being built; it would be handy for her in the future. 'I knew Corny Dowley,' she said, and Tom could tell from the way she said it that she knew who he was, that she knew Corny Dowley had killed his father. She wouldn't give you tuppence for Dowley, she said. 'A right eejit, that fellow.' The woman was sorry for him, trying to be good to him, but even so she didn't suggest he should climb up beside her on the cart.

He thought about that while she talked to him. 'Keep well away from that fellow,' Dorrie Deavy's father would have said. The Deavy boys crossed the street when they saw him approaching; he'd seen them doing it. His grandmother had been going to kiss him that day, only she'd changed her mind like Mr Coyne had. Deso Furphy and Neck Daly only bothered with him because they were curious about him.

'I never thought I'd see a bridge,' the woman on the cart said. 'Isn't it a wonder what they can do?'

He agreed it was. He had never before thought of his mother like that, out in a field with her clothes half off. He'd only pretended to understand when Holy Mullihan went on about saying prayers to cleanse him. It was why all of them were keen on making him touch the holy clay.

The woman said goodbye, shaking the reins to hurry the donkey up as it turned away on to the track that led to her cottage. In the distance Tom could hear the voices of the men working at the bridge, and when it came into sight he saw that it now extended over fourteen of the iron supports. Three lorries, empty of their loads, filled the air with dust as slowly they drove away. 'A fellow at Confession,' was how a joke of Neck Daly's went. ' "Father, I sinned: I rode a woman from Carrigtohill." "Well," says the Father, "isn't anything better than walking?" D'you understand that, Tom? D'you get the meaning of it?'

His grandmother would be frightened to be in a room with him, which was why they couldn't go and see her in her house; his grandfather would be frightened to be near him at all. 'We've mongrels enough,' he'd heard Mr O'Hagan complaining, kicking at a dog that had climbed up on another one by Mr Coyne's petrol pump. Mongrels were any old dogs, sometimes peculiar-looking, the street-corner curs that gathered dust and fleas, carelessly born also. 'God takes back a soul,' Holy Mullihan said; a soul was only on loan. There was a man out in the hills beyond the town who had a terrible disease, a man who lived alone in a hovel, blinded in both his eyes, hardly able to walk.

Holy Mullihan said he was like that because he'd been born in sin.

*

Hearing the sound of his returning footsteps on the gravel sweep, Villana turned down the page of her novel and with her cigarettes and lighter in one hand went to greet her husband. She poured him sherry. She made him tell her about his day. She listened to the detail of disputes that had arisen, and to his courthouse gossip. She was restless until, once more, he touched upon her girlish beauty and what it meant to him.

*

Letters came for John James. They were letters of apology, all of which he burnt without reading a second time. In passing, the money was mentioned, a statement to the effect that it didn't matter, that between friends money never did. But in subsequent letters the sum referred to appeared to matter more. Attention was drawn to the circumstances of its withdrawal from the Munster and Leinster Bank, to its time in the hat-box, to its eventual arrival on the island. A loan had been agreed, one letter in particular stated, though no arrangement had been made for how it might be repaid, and in what manner.

John James swore. He cursed the woman. His leg ached. No loan had been agreed; the banknotes had been foisted on him in public, the cause of acute embarrassment. Clearly he would have to return the money since he had no claim to it. Clearly he had no option but to make another journey to the boarding-house. Without quite knowing why he did so, he waited until a Monday afternoon came round again.

'Oh, honey! Oh, my darling boy!' She wept as soon as she saw him. The apologies that had been written down poured again from her lips. She would kneel before him if he

(168)

required it. She had suffered a sunstroke that day, she wouldn't have spoilt the wedding occasion for worlds.

He attempted to count the banknotes into her hands, so that there could be no argument afterwards. He tried to be exact and businesslike, but the notes dropped to the floor and he was obliged to go down on his hands and knees to retrieve them. As soon as he stood up again he felt an arm around his waist. He shook it off, insisting that he had come on a commercial matter, but somehow or other he found himself on the way upstairs, and then she was saying that she forgave him, that it was a terrible way to behave, not replying to a person's letters, especially after a person had been taken ill. She sprinkled eau de Cologne on to her sheets, telling him not to be silly when he shook his head.

*

Carriglas, October 16th, 1931. Sunshine glances over harvest stubble, petals fall in the garden. The apples have been picked, the air smells softly of the season. Almost as though they've made a mistake, the strawberry trees blossom, then Michaelmas daisies come.

'You never forget,' he said this afternoon, taking the can of tea from me in the orchard, where old trees are being felled. He hesitated, again as though about to say something, but in the end he did not.

*

For just a few moments Mrs Rolleston forgot that Villana had married the solicitor, and wondered why he was reading a newspaper in the drawing-room. People had always come and gone at Carriglas, servants and visitors, friends, relations, painters and wallpaper-hangers, friends of other friends, the man to repair the banister-rail. Sarah Pollexfen had come. She'd come herself. Linchy had come.

She closed her eyes. The chaffinch flew about the

drawing-room, she tore the paper into scraps. 'Come and get the rabbits,' her son said, and in the little study Villana lifted the shotgun from the wall. With her eyes still closed, she remembered the wedding preparations, the wedding itself: events and statements came swiftly back to her, and she chided herself for her silliness in forgetting that Villana had married the solicitor.

'The shreds of summer left,' she remarked. 'The nicer side of winter just arriving.'

They listened to her, books and cigarettes for a moment laid down. They honoured her age, they showed a suitable respect: she'd brought them up to that. The solicitor's newspaper was on his knees, Sarah Pollexfen's embroidery idle.

'October is my favourite month of autumn,' Villana obligingly responded. Her husband concurred, devoting consideration to a survey of the autumn months. November he liked less, he said.

'I should like arrangements made for the disposal of my jewellery,' she informed them. 'I shall be parted from it soon in any case.'

They did not care for that. The finely wrought Rolleston brows of her grandchildren frowned. They did not meet her gaze. They did not wish to have this conversation.

'Oh, now,' Villana said.

But since she had begun, since she had become entangled in the subject, it was certainly better to continue. 'I do not wish to distress you, Villana, nor anyone else. I am simply endeavouring to converse. Old women die in the night, you know.'

She did not know if she loved her grandchildren any more, and rather thought she did not, and had not for many years. She felt she had been damaged and considered that unfair, since she was, after all, only their grandmother, not their mother.

'Send to Cork,' she said, her tone peremptory, 'for a man

to come to value what there is. Accept any offer that is not a swindle.'

'There is no need,' John James began. 'Really there is no need.'

'Well yes, there is. As a matter of fact there is, you know.' And she explained that the motor-car which the garage man had apparently earmarked for the family should be purchased. 'You will not be made use of,' she reassured the solicitor. 'Villana has said you were not married for your possessions.'

She made that clear in case Villana had not said it herself to him, for Villana was often careless. In childhood it had been the same.

'There is another thing, since we are talking on the subject and since in fact we have our own solicitor in the room. Provision must be made for that child.'

Again they did not like it. John James spoke, attempting to placate her, she supposed: she did not listen. 'You are in charge now,' his father used to say each time he went away to join the regiment, but John James wasn't the sort to be in charge. John James, she'd often thought, should have been a travelling salesman.

'The child,' Villana began, but feeling it to be her privilege she interrupted her. She did not trust Villana in this matter. She did not trust John James. And Lionel would give in to pressure. The picnic was over, she thought; twilight was giving way to darkness. She liked the sound of that and wanted to repeat the observation aloud, but did not do so.

'Wait please, Villana.' She turned her look upon the solicitor, offering him a smile that once had upset the demeanours of younger men. 'Finnamore, will you see that papers are drawn up?'

'Concerning the estate, Mrs Rolleston? I can assure you I am proceeding with considerable alacrity. The law, un-fortunately, cannot be pressed beyond its natural pace.

But certainly advances are being made.'

'I do not mean concerning the estate. If Villana has not told you yet she will tell you soon — there is no point whatsoever in your snatching back those forgotten acres.'

'I do not seek to snatch, Mrs Rolleston. Only to regain what is rightly the family's due.'

'Will you see that papers are drawn up, Finnamore, that ensure provision is made for the gate-lodge child?'

'Yes, of course. If that is your wish. As to the other work — '

'Such a child is often kept hidden, you know. It was I who insisted otherwise years ago. We therefore have an obligation.'

He seemed nonplussed, but even so he nodded and she was glad of that. Again she closed her eyes for a moment, for she felt her breathing quicken, and thought to rest them for a moment. The solicitor's voice continued, informing her of irrelevancies.

'You understand, Finnamore, how that child's father died? My granddaughter has explained?'

'Indeed. I am quite conversant, I believe.'

Once upon a time, of course, there'd been another child: Villana might not have told him that, either. They none of them might ever have spoken to a soul, keeping all of it to themselves, as their childhood habit had been. A day would come, some time in the future, when nobody would know, when the truth would be buried and lie like some forgotten treasure in the ground.

'I hope you will accept,' she said to the solicitor, 'that you have a duty in all this? You are a clever man. You are cleverer than the Rollestons.'

'There is no need for this!' Villana suddenly cried out, anger causing her to stammer slightly. 'Finnamore must not be spoken to in this way.'

'I do not speak to him in any way in particular. By saying clever, I do not insult him. You worry when you are old,

Finnamore, that the innocent are punished. It is enough that poor Linchy died in error.'

Her hands, resting lightly on the arms of her chair, now pushed her to her feet. Sarah Pollexfen moved in some manner, as though to offer assistance. Lionel moved forward too. But assistance was not necessary, and they should have known it.

'Be certain, Finnamore, that my granddaughter has explained the circumstances of our butler's death. I would ask you to be certain. That is a personal wish.'

It was too simple just to say it was her grandchildren's flesh and bones that should have been scattered all over the avenue. It was easy to avoid the heart of the matter, though naturally people would want to.

'Naturally,' she repeated.

No one commented. She had thought John James or Villana would make further protestations, but no one said a thing. Sarah Pollexfen remained where she stood, having sensed the rejection of her assistance. Lionel stared at a rug on the floor. John James leaned against the wall between two of the French windows. Villana played with her cigarette-lighter.

She thought she saw the solicitor's lips move, no doubt wishing to acknowledge her requests, to affirm in his solicitor's manner, not giving too much away. He had crossed the room and stood stiffly beside her granddaughter's chair. She had made them all unhappy, she thought, and they were glad to see her go, being fearful of what she might say next.

'Forgive me,' she begged, but her voice was so tired she wondered if they could hear it. She raised it with an effort. Only the gate-lodge child mattered now, she said. Only he was important, since he was their inheritor.

*

Carriglas, October 27th, 1931. In the drawing-room the pages of the Irish Times *rustled as John James turned them.*

There was the sound of the flint sparking in Villana's cigarette-lighter. No one spoke. Mr Balt seemed awkward and upset, as puzzled as I was myself, both of us beyond the family pale. Since their marriage Villana has been attentive to him in a way I had hardly thought she would be, fussing over how his eggs are cooked and his clothes ironed. 'Finnamore,' he has said to me. 'You must call me Finnamore, for I should like to call you Sarah.' I must remember that. I must address him as Finnamore, though I know I shall continue to write Mr Balt in my diary and I shall always think of him as Mr Balt. Of that I'm certain.

Later tonight, as I passed the door of the nursery-schoolroom, I heard his voice raised. 'But nothing could,' he urgently exclaimed. 'Nothing on earth could ever change my feelings for you.' There was a murmur in reply, and with greater passion than before he repeated this confirmation of his attachment.

In my bedroom, as now I write, I hear again the old woman's insistent voice rambling on about the butler's death and provision for the gate-lodge child. Through a flicker of lamplight Villana glances away, as though seeking solace in the shadowy flowers of the garden. John James sighs. And in Lionel's eyes there is such pain as I have never seen before in a human face.

Carriglas, November 22nd, 1931. The man came today to make an offer for Mrs Rolleston's jewellery. It was accepted on her insistence.

Carriglas, November 27th, 1931. 'You have made provision?' she said at dinner, addressing her grandson-in-law. 'You have seen to my wishes?' He replied that the matter had been discussed with her grandchildren, and then proceeded to go into detail as to the agreement reached. She cut him short. She did not wish to hear, she stated sharply. 'In no way do I distrust you, Finnamore,' she added later on.

Carriglas, November 30th, 1931. 'I beg you,' I said. 'I beg you to tell me.' I could not prevent those words. It was,

(174)

indeed, all I could do to prevent myself from saying more, from confessing that I had loved him since the day he'd complimented me on the tennis-court. I waited, looking at him, willing him to speak to me. He smiled and only said, most sadly: 'Dear Sarah. Dear, generous Sarah.'

9. Tom and Mrs Rolleston

Tom waited for Sister Conheady to appear. The linoleum of the floor had been waxed that morning and the smell of polish was still in the air. It was never warm in the room, and the glass-paned bookcase doors were never unlocked when the lay sister showed him in to wait for Sister Conheady. He wondered how many books there were. He wondered who else ever borrowed them. He'd never seen another person in the room.

'Ah, Tom, where'd we be without you?' Sister Conheady said, soundlessly arriving. Her grasp of the doorhandle, and the movement of the door itself, had not betrayed her entrance: only her greeting ever did that. She unlocked the bookcase and then the drawer where she kept her red exercise-book.

'Has she read *Darkened Rooms*? D'you remember that name?'

He examined the title, printed in ink on the brown-paper cover; he opened the book. *By Philip Gibbs*, it said inside.

'That's not one I've brought over,' he said.

Sister Conheady replaced on a shelf the book he had returned to her. *Miss V. Rolleston*, she wrote in the red exercise-book, and then made a cross sound with her tongue. She corrected the entry to *Mrs. V. Balt*. It was the eighth time she'd made that slip. Tom had counted.

'Now,' she said, handing the book to him.

As he received it, he tried to touch her fingers with his, to see if she'd draw them away. He didn't manage to do so because she was holding the other side of the book. He wondered if she was holding it there on purpose, because a nun had to be extra careful.

'You get used to writing down a name,' she said, which was what she'd said on the seven previous occasions. 'Is Mrs Balt well these days?'

'I think she is.'

'Bring her this one too. I have it put by in the drawer for her.'

Again there was a chance to discover if she would permit his hand to touch hers. *Out of the Ruins*, he read on the cover of the book she handed him. But she held it in the same way, the fingers grasping it well away from his.

She locked the glass-paned door, and then she locked the drawer where she kept the red exercise-book and the books she sometimes put aside. He liked the smell of cloth that always came from her, and the way it rustled sometimes, and the way her beads jangled when she reached up to a high shelf. Deso Furphy said a nun had no hair on her head.

'Sister Conheady,' he said, 'would you be frightened to touch me?'

Her high, smooth forehead, a shade less white than the wimple that framed it, wrinkled immediately. The empty eyes, that had never in his presence betrayed emotion, clouded perceptibly. A hand searched for the beads that hung within the folds of her habit.

'To touch you, Tom?'

'Because of the way I am.'

She did not move. She stood by the bookcase, with her back pressed into it. The agitation in her face increased. Tom could sense her telling him to go away, even though she didn't say it. He didn't want to go away. He wanted to explain that he had understood why people thought of him like that ever since he'd seen Briscoe with the girl, Briscoe trying to do what Mr O'Hagan had kicked the dog

(178)

for. He wanted to tell Sister Conheady about Dorrie Deavy repeating what her father had said, and how Mr Coyne had changed his mind about inviting him into his house, and how his grandmother had been going to kiss him and then hadn't. He wanted to tell her that people didn't object to being in a room with him, that only the Deavy boys moved to the other side of the street. The woman on the cart had been sorry for him but she didn't want to contaminate herself. He began again about Briscoe and the girl, how Briscoe's coat had been lying beside them on the grass.

'What are you talking about?' She crossed herself. He mustn't say that, she said. She told him to go to Confession. She asked him if he was looking after the holy well.

'I keep an eye on it all right.'

'When you put your hand down into the clay keep it there for a long while. Don't talk about those other things.'

He could see that she was praying. Her lips weren't moving, no sound came from her, but he was aware that she was interceding for him. When he guessed she had finished he said:

'I only wanted to ask you.'

'As soon as you'll get across to the island go up to that place and put your hand down into the moisture. Say your rosary there.'

'Yes,' he said.

He began to go away, but she called him back when he'd reached the door and told him to wait there a minute. She opened the drawer and took out the exercise-book. She tore a page out and wrote on it, then searched impatiently for an envelope. Failing to find one, she folded the page several times and wrote on the outside of it. 'Give that to Mrs Balt,' she said. 'Put it inside one of the books, only draw her attention to it. Don't forget now.'

'I'm sorry I said that to you.'

Sister Conheady did not reply. Her head was bowed, and he left the room not knowing if the agitation had gone from her face. In the hall the Reverend Mother was unhurriedly pacing up and down, talking quietly to a young nun Tom had never seen before. Engrossed in their conversation, they didn't speak to him as he went by. He reached up and unlatched the door, and closed it softly behind him.

'How're you doing, Tom?' Mr Coyne said as he passed the petrol pump, and he replied that he was doing all right. All the way to the quays there wasn't a chance to read the note Sister Conheady had written because someone might have seen him at it and guessed he was doing something wrong. On the ferryboat he wasn't able to read it in front of the ferryman, but on the island, when he was out of sight of the boat, he lifted the two books from his schoolbag and took the note from where he'd placed it between the pages of one of them. *Please in future send one of the maids for the books*, Sister Conheady's handwriting instructed, nothing else.

He replaced the note between the pages of *Out of the Ruins* and walked on, passing the gate-lodge by because he always delivered the library books to the kitchen of the house as soon as he'd collected them. He should have known something as bad as this would happen if he was outspoken with Sister Conheady. 'That'll be the first one you'll read yourself,' she'd said once, taking a book down from the shelves, and reading a few lines about a shipwreck.

In the kitchen of the house he wanted to tell his mother what had happened, but he knew she'd be cross so he didn't. He placed the books on the table as he always did, and placed the note on top of them so that it would be seen. His mother called out from the sculleries, asking if it was Tom who had come in.

'I'm leaving the books here, and a note Sister Conheady wrote.'

'Tom, Mrs Rolleston wants you. Will you go up to her bedroom?'

It would be to buy another postal order. He thought that

all the way up the back stairs, imagining Mr O'Hagan's face in the post office and the way he had of whispering to himself while he slowly leafed through the box of postal orders.

'Ah, Tom.'

'Hullo, Mrs Rolleston.'

She was in bed, sitting up against her pillows. She smiled at him. She pointed at the money on the dressing-table, the envelope already addressed beside it. When he was over at the convent tomorrow, she began, and did not have to continue because he understood.

'Tom,' she said when he was about to go. 'Come here beside me, Tom.'

He crossed to her bedside and stood there. She looked at him with a trace of a smile on her lips, her eyes brighter than he had ever noticed them before, her cheeks more lined and sunken than he had ever noticed them either.

'Tom,' she said again, and to his astonishment she held her arms out, wanting him to come closer to her. She repeated his name, and then he felt the wrinkled skin of her face on his cheek, and her lips kissing him, as softly and as warmly as his mother did when she said goodnight. Her hands held on to his shoulders, her grasp tightened around him. 'Say goodbye to me, Tom,' she whispered, but he didn't say anything, fearing that if he did she'd let him go.

*

In the dark of another night, thoughts and memories mingled. They ran about and would not flow together. Sunshine was warm on her forehead. She watched her breath on the chill air. She heard her laughter when two men on horseback rode among the furniture of the drawing-room, two rakes from Mallow or wherever. A band played in the alcove on the stairs, her own feet danced. *Only I had bad luck a week ago*, the familiar loops of Kathleen Quigley's handwriting reminded her.

As fragile as the veins of a fallen leaf, all of it would be shattered by the same idle touch that had reached for her husband and her son and her grandchildren's mother, for Linchy, and for Dowley in the end. *Wouldn't you wonder how a person could get the way Corny Dowley was when he could have made some girl a decent husband? But I'm telling you the truth saying there's no hard feelings. There's no one doesn't know you were always goodness itself to Kathleen Quigley.* He had lain in wait at Lahane cross-roads, for men whom in other times he might have smoked a cigarette with. He had lain in wait on the billiard-hall steps, and become the victim of his own trap. His mother walked out into the sea on the day of his funeral.

A fire burned in the bedroom, as it always did during the winter months. The lamp on the dressing-table cast a soft, yellow light. For more than seventy years she had slept in this room. The son she had outlived had been conceived and born here. Her tears had dampened the yielding warmth of the bed she lay down in now, tears of pleasure often. 'I'm so sorry, Brigid,' she tried to comfort when Brigid had wept also. 'I'm so very sorry.' The remains had lain with a sheet drawn over them, one sheet replaced by another because the blood still oozed. *Mightn't it appease the conscience if you sent a few shillings?* But conscience had stayed to mock, and to insist upon as its greater due.

'Mrs Rolleston.'

Sarah Pollexfen stood with a lamp in the open doorway. 'You said to come and say goodnight.'

'Did I? D'you know, I'd quite forgotten that.'

'I woke you. I'm very sorry.'

'No, you didn't, not at all. Sit down, Sarah. Sit where I can see you. We have not talked to one another for years.'

From her bed she watched while the lamp was placed on the dressing-table, not close to the one that was no longer alight but on the other side of the ornate looking-glass. Sarah Pollexfen sat within the glow the single lamp threw, her back to the scent bottles and the ivory hairbrushes of the dressing-table, her fingers touching on her lap.

'The wretched journey to a woman's bed, the empty marriage, guilt begetting guilt. Sarah, do you understand?'

She must have closed her eyes because when she opened them she saw that Sarah Pollexfen was shaking her head. She said she wanted it written down. She wanted it in Sarah Pollexfen's diaries, so that the truth could be passed on. Or left behind, whichever way you looked at it.

'They terrified him, Sarah. Day after day, all summer long, they hunted that child as an animal is hunted.'

*

Carriglas, December 12th, 1931. Earlier, that morning, she had told me of a dream: about being in a gondola in Venice on her honeymoon and how the gondola had become the boat, bedecked with ribbons, that took her back to the island which was to be her home. One after another, she shook the servants' hands on the steps of the house. 'All that you found lovely about Carriglas was lovely for me too, Sarah.' There was no ferryboat then; when people fell ill on the island they came to the house and the house looked after them. She described the town as it had been, its business premises thriving, the pretty bandstand given by the Rollestons to decorate the promenade.

But when I sat with her in the evening her mood was different. I knew, of course, about the occurrence that appeared to haunt her. After all, I had been here at the time. And I, too, had been angry with the children.

'"Come and get the rabbits," their father used to say when they were tiny. And then he'd lift Villana up so that she could reach the shotgun down from the wall. Off they'd go, he and his children.'

'It's best forgotten, Mrs Rolleston. It's all too long ago.'

Her breathing softened; her eyes closed. Gently I put

more logs on the fire and when they blazed up my own eyes faltered also. For a minute or two I dozed.

'I have dreamed too often of that red-haired child. Too often, Sarah.'

Her voice woke me. She paused and then she spoke again, asking me if I, too, dreamed about what I had sought to banish from my memory years ago. I shook my head, but as I did so all that had distressed me then returned. The red-haired child ran over heather and rocks, chased out of a hovel that smelt of turf smoke and potatoes boiling. His feet were bare, his jersey ragged. He ran as swiftly as a hare.

'Did you ever know, Sarah, that his father had long ago gone from the island to find a passage to America? A half-witted uncle – Drunk Paddy they call him now – shared that hovel with the child and his mother. God knows what became of the father, a lot of them just disappeared.'

'Mrs Rolleston, all this is over and done with. It's really best forgotten.'

'My grandchildren hunted a child, Sarah. My grandchildren and your brother. As of right, they hunted. They were the children of Carriglas.'

I rose and moved across the room. I took her hands, hoping my touch would shake her melancholy off. But she repeated what she had said already, her voice unwavering and strong. I knew the details she pressed so urgently upon me. I did not want to hear them.

'Shall I fetch you something warm? Milk? Or cocoa?'

'As soon as their father returned to the regiment the shotgun was taken from the wall. As soon as there were only two women to deceive.'

'They did not realise. Children often don't.'

'How often, that summer, did the thought of their game excite Villana while she recited her poetry for you in the nursery-schoolroom, or bent her head over the sums you set? Do you wonder about that, Sarah? Do you lie awake and wonder?'

I placed her hands beneath the bedclothes, and settled her pillows. As I returned to the fire, goose pimples ran over my arms and legs. In a moment she said:

'One of them drove him on to where another waited. His feet bled on the gorse he ran through. He stumbled and fell down. Is that as you have seen it, too? In dreams, Sarah?'

I did not reply. I steadied a shaking in my hands by pressing them into my thighs. It was not something I had ever dreamed about.

'Exhausted among the rocks, his fearful tears, the shotgun aimed. Is that what you have seen, Sarah? And have you heard the children's laughter?'

'Of course I haven't.' My voice rose, almost shrill in the quiet room. 'You punished the children. They understood.'

'Yet they did not obey me. They obeyed neither of us, Sarah.'

'Mrs Rolleston, do please try to rest. No matter how it was, it belongs to the past now.'

'The past has no belongings. The past does not obligingly absorb what is not wanted.'

Did I excuse it still? she asked me. Did I call it a sport for a summer's day and excuse it because those summer days were long ago? I would have given anything I possessed to make her cease, but she murmured on, wandering back through the years of her life, rambling sometimes in what she said, but always returning to the red-haired child.

'What did they do to him that summer, Sarah?'

'Please don't talk like this, Mrs Rolleston. Please. I beg you.'

She paid me no attention. She had no interest in my answers, even though she asked me questions. She was aware of little in her bedroom except that someone of my name was there.

'What monstrousness was bred in him that summer, Sarah?'

It was I who had seen the children returning to the garden with the shotgun. I had run towards them in agitation, knowing the weapon should not have been taken from the study in their father's absence. 'Don't tell Grandmamma,' Villana had pleaded, and then Hugh appeared and I knew he had been with them. 'Sarah, we were only playing,' he said, but none of them told me what their game had been. It was Haverty, afterwards, who did that, asking me to speak to them. Later, when my remonstrances proved ineffective, he complained to Mrs Rolleston that their game was continuing.

She murmured from her sleep and soon afterwards her eyes opened. She sighed, a whispering exhalation that hardly stirred the silence. A moment later she said:

'How convenient revolution is for men like Cornelius Dowley! What balm for the bitter heart!'

I did not understand, and when I tried to think I felt my mind oppressed. Cornelius Dowley had to do with the tragedy on the avenue, and with the bridge that was being built. We had been talking about the children.

'There are moments you cannot ever forget, Sarah. No matter how long you live. I stood there in the dawn, waiting for them to return from their party, and heard their voices on the sea. When I spoke they guessed immediately. "Dowley," John James said.'

No one had ever told me this. No one had ever even faintly hinted. I heard her saying that Linchy's murder belonged in a thread of carnage that was unbearable even to think about. She mused to herself. I could not hear, until she said:

'I don't know why I send that woman money except, perhaps, to buy more pain. For what on earth would it matter if people knew that a childhood cruelty has turned around and damned a household?'

'I did not ever know.' I meant to continue but did not do so. Instead, again, I asked her to rest, repeating my offer to

fetch her cocoa or warm milk. I begged her to say no more tonight. She paid me no heed.

'When those brutes of soldiers shot down Dowley they came over to tell us. Delighted with themselves.'

'Mrs Rolleston – '

'As of right again, Dowley had been hunted, this time to the kill. That same week the engagement was broken off.'

I felt myself shaking my head without knowing why I was doing so. I tried to contradict without knowing what I was contradicting. I said my brother and Villana had been engaged and then decided not to be. It was a usual thing to happen.

'No, Sarah. No, not at all. Your brother and Villana turned away from all they felt for one another, and perhaps they had to. For how could their children play in that same garden and not ever be told of what had festered so horribly in a wound? How could the reason for the tragedy on the avenue not ever be revealed? Was it to be kept from them that the cornering of Cornelius Dowley on the steps of a billiard-hall was an irony and a repetition? Was it to be kept from them that his mother walked out into the waves? And that all of it began in the idyll of a lazy summer?'

Her voice went on, speaking now of fate; how her grandchildren and my brother, in luckier circumstances, would have escaped their conscience. Chance had supplied a gruesome plot: in another place and another time they would have grown up healthily to exorcise their aberrations by shrugging them away. She lost the thread of what she was trying to communicate, was incoherent, then spoke again of Dowley's mother walking into the sea.

'Can you imagine her, Sarah? That tormented woman begging for the sea's oblivion? Her husband gone and now her son. Life with a half-wit in a hovel was what she faced. How much nicer, Sarah, the future was for me!'

Again coherence went. She spoke of the dogs there'd been at Carriglas in her time. And then about the day a chaffinch had flown about the drawing-room, and the day the family had posed for the silver-framed photograph in the hall, and the day she'd been glad Lionel was declared unfit for service in the war. Time had tamed the Rollestons, who had come to the island with slaughter in their wake, but time could not be trusted.

'It never just passes, Sarah. It is always on one side or the other. Women huddled in their corners, children begged, men disappeared. Would their time ever come? How could it come? And yet it did.'

How often, that summer, had I convinced myself it was nothing worse than taking out a boat without permission, or climbing the dead tree in the hillfield? How often had I said to myself, as I had to Mrs Rolleston just now, that children don't realise? 'Your father will be ashamed of you,' I'd crossly reminded them, 'and I am too.' Their grandmother had meted out the sternest punishment she could devise; I'd made Hugh promise separately that nothing like this would ever happen again. In the end, after their initial disobedience, they'd been contrite, all four of them. Their high spirits had been abandoned for a quieter charm; the household returned to normal. When, later, the episode was retailed to Colonel Rolleston, as it had to be, there were silent mealtimes, and gifts, brought back to Carriglas, were not given. Then the pall of disapproval lifted. In retrospect, at the Misses Goodbody's and in Dunadry Rectory, I convinced myself again that children are wild and often primitive. I did not believe there was some extra wickedness in the children of Carriglas, some harshness beneath the attractions of the surface. I did not think of the misdemeanour as 'hunting a child' and I don't believe, at that time, Mrs Rolleston did either. The shadow of that summer faded beneath my own insistence that it should; and no doubt it did so for her too.

'Am I right in what I say, Sarah, about another place and another time?'

I did not answer because I did not, any more, know how to. The rambling whisper began again, ceased, and was again renewed. A silence became prolonged.

'Please look after them, Sarah. Please don't desert us.'

I moved to the bedside, and reassured her. The myrtles and the little hebes must be protected when the first hard frosts of January came. It was always she who had remembered that. Her voice, speaking still of the garden, dwindled and then gathered strength again. She would remain in her bedroom now. She would not ever again go outside, she sensed that in her bones. She would not again descend the stairs, to the kitchen or the dining-room. But what she waited for would not come quickly: she sensed that too.

*

A small crowd, composed mainly of tinker children, stood in a perishing wind while the courage of Cornelius Dowley was recalled. Brother Meagher was there, and the men who had been Cornelius Dowley's companions eleven years ago at Lahane crossroads. Attention was drawn to the carved inscription, in both Irish and English, that gave the dates of birth and death, and praised a hero's gallantry. The bridge was blessed, as Holy Mullihan had said it would be. The engineer and the surveyor who had worked together on the project were present, though more to satisfy themselves with a final inspection than to take part in the modest ceremony. The workmen who had set the girders in concrete beneath the surface of the water, who had laid the bridge's surface down and built the pillars at either end, were clearing out ditches by a road to the west of the town.

Tom ran back across the bridge when everyone had gone. He'd seen Brother Meagher looking at him, the straight line of his eyebrows bisecting his face below the forehead. Brother Meagher considered he should not be there: Tom even thought he had observed an involuntary gesture of the Christian Brother's hand, the hand flicked dismissively backwards as a signal that he should go away, and then the gesture checked. 'When you come to the Brothers',' Holy Mullihan had predicted, 'Brother Meagher will be keeping an eye on you. It would be his duty, Tom.'

Soon it would be Christmas. Always on Christmas Day Tom went up to the house and had his dinner in the kitchen. In the middle of it Mrs Rolleston came down with presents for his mother and himself and for anyone else in the kitchen. There were sprigs of holly on the dresser, and plum pudding that his mother made. It was dark when they went down the avenue to the gate-lodge.

But this year it would be different. His mother had said it would because Mrs Rolleston no longer came downstairs. Tom didn't think he'd see her again, but he often thought of her, in her armchair by the window in her room. She wouldn't bother with the postal orders any more, he imagined.

In the gate-lodge Tom sat close to the range, warming his hands on the hot metal. It was too cold to go to the saint's place; they didn't want him today in the kitchen or the sculleries.

'Tom!' Patty's voice called, and then she pushed open the door from the yard, in her hand the *Irish Times* she'd been sent down to the pier to collect. 'How're you doing, Tom?'

She sat with him, warming herself too. After St Stephen's Day the ferryboat wouldn't make the journey any more, the ferryman had told her. It was the only news she had, so they talked about that.

10. Sarah Departs

___

'I'll take them downstairs,' Patty says in the pink-distempered bedroom where Sarah's death has taken place and where her diaries are stacked beneath the window-shelf.

'Did she want them destroyed, Patty?'

'She only said we could when we had read them. If we wanted to.'

Tom nods. Both of them are saddened by their loss. There was a tidiness about the household as it had become: for the last few years it has seemed right that there should be the three of them, the family gone and its attendants left.

'She had a lovely hand,' Patty remarks as she gathers up the diaries. Already some entries have been read. Patty has a picture in her mind which she did not have before: of the plain child growing up in a cheerless rectory, of a teacher in a boarding-school, of a woman painfully in love. In the kitchen she releases the pulley that keeps the drying-rack suspended, and picks the garments off it one by one. Folding each as she does so, she stacks them ready for ironing. It is odd, she thinks, that Sarah Pollexfen should have wanted all that to be known.

In the town on the mainland, people learn of the death. Esmeralda, youngest of the Coyne daughters, hears the news in Meath's, while filling a wire basket with groceries. It will make a difference, she considers. Tom will be affected: it will be Tom's house now, just as the land is

Tom's. Mr O'Hagan hears the news and remembers Sarah Pollexfen entering the kitchen with a tray while he and the ferryman toasted Villana Rolleston on her wedding day. Sister Conheady, who suffered a stroke a month ago, attempts to cross herself but cannot. Her face has frozen into a tranquil smile which does not reflect the nature of her thoughts. I was uncharitable, her thoughts accuse. She should have given the child the books and only smiled, never writing what she did: she envies Sarah Pollexfen her release. 'God rest the soul,' Mrs Moledy remarks to the postman who rings her bell to inform her, knowing she has had a connection with the family. Mrs Moledy – a great age now – lives in the basement flat of what used to be her boarding-house, which she sold in 1959 to an insurance company. Two streets away, in the offices of Harbinson and Balt, Eugene Prille attends to the sparse legalities that the death necessitates.

Her skin tightens in the pink-distempered bedroom, her blood is as cold as water. The rictus that shadows the slackened jaw is pressed away by the woman who has come to lay the body out. Familiar obsequies are observed, arrangements made.

'A good soul,' the undertaker murmurs on the way upstairs to take his measurements.

'Yes, she was that.'

Tom's black hair is brushed back now, touched here and there with grey; his childhood fringe has gone. The face that was round in childhood and once resembled his mother's is irregular, its skin toughened from exposure to the weather. But his eyes have retained the innocence that was there in the past, contributing to the youthfulness that persists in his agility as he goes about his work in the fields.

'Well, that's it,' the undertaker remarks, with professional finality.

'Thanks for coming over.'

Together they leave the room, joined on the landing by

Tom's black terrier. They descend the curving staircase, where family portraits still hang. The corpse will remain in the bedroom until an hour before the funeral, since that has always been the family way.

'That's a bitter wind,' the undertaker conversationally observes as they pass through the hall-door and stand for a moment on the steps.

'She hated cold,' Tom recalls. 'She often said it.'

Later, other people learn of the death of the Rollestons' poor relation, and note from the newspaper obituary the date and the time of the funeral. In Unionhall the sons of the Camiers who attended Villana Rolleston's wedding display no interest in the death. In Buttevant a granddaughter of Lady Rossboyne tries to remember who Sarah Pollexfen was but cannot. In England the children of Sarah Pollexfen's brother telephone each other to say that the aunt they have never met has apparently died in the house they'd always heard so much about, on an island off the coast of Co. Cork. 'I am too old for funerals now,' Villiers Hadnett says in the house he inherited near Athlone. 'Treacherous things, funerals.' And in Unionhall and Buttevant and England no plans are made to attend the funeral, either.

In the kitchen, during the days that pass, the perusal of the diaries continues: a solemn task, since last wishes come into it. And the revelations that were not allowed in a lifetime continue also, though often the ground is familiar.

Carriglas, January 18th, 1938. We have painted the conservatory. John James brought back putty and Villana and I pressed it in with kitchen knives. I never thought we could do it, but Villana said of course we could.

Carriglas, March 9th, 1947. A portrait on the staircase wall fell in the night, splinters of glass everywhere. Both frame and canvas are damaged and John James says there is no one in the vicinity who could properly restore them. So we have taken the picture to one of the visitors' rooms, leaning it against the wall in the long cupboard.

Carriglas, June 14th, 1953. For two days Lionel and Haverty and Tom have been trying to repair the water-ram and in the meanwhile we have had no water in the house. But this evening it began to trickle again.

Carriglas, November 3rd, 1968. 'D'you remember my sick hen?' Villana suddenly said at dinner, and in fact I did not at first remember and had to think for several minutes. Damp has spread on the ceiling of the bedroom that was Mrs Rolleston's. Patty and I moved the dressing-table from beneath it. I put away the ivory hairbrushes and the scent bottles, which have remained there since December 1931. I wonder if anyone will ever use that scent again. Perhaps one day there will be an auction in this house, and someone then may buy these small remains.

As a tapestry of domestic detail, the years that separate Tom and Patty from 1931 are spread before them in the record that has been kept. In other upstairs rooms bed-clothes are taken from the mattresses, furniture covered. A crack occurs in the cast-iron of the kitchen range. Villana drives the big black Renault, its hood drawn back in summer. Haverty climbs on to the roof to install an aerial for a wireless set; one autumn night a strawberry tree slumps against its neighbour. There are references to the Shannon Scheme of electrification, to Lionel's wartime crop of sugar beet, to the snow of 1946. Arthritis affects John James's leg. In the drawing-room the piano Miss de Ryal played on the afternoon of the wedding slips out of tune. Dawn lightens yet another sky. Curtains are drawn against another night, and then another.

There is hardly a word that is not easily read, no error of spelling or grammar remains uncorrected. The handwriting is like the woman: the flow of prose recalls her also. Patty has forgotten that when first she came to Carriglas she assumed Sarah Pollexfen to be Villana's sister, until Brigid explained that she was not. Neither Patty nor Tom has known of her attachment to Lionel. Sarah Pollexfen was a woman who went about the house; her story, of duty and unrequited love, was shaped by other people's greater claims. They never saw her angry or emotional. Yet in her diaries she wrote about her naked body.

Affected by these memories, they reflect upon their own. They remember the night of the Zodiacs, how Patty had heard about the entertainment and Tom had gone to it. Tom remembers Derek Birthistle banished to the cloakroom during catechism, and Neck Daly and Deso Furphy giving the Mussolini salute in South Main Street, and the ebony ruler of Brother Meagher furiously rapping the blackboard. The first picture Patty ever saw in Traynor's Picture Palace was *The Girl of the Golden West*. 'I never use the old cycle,' Haverty said, and showed Tom how to oil the hubs and the chain, and how to raise and lower the saddle and handlebars. 'They eat meat themselves on a Friday,' Brigid explained when Patty had been at Carriglas a week. 'I'll fry you an egg.' Clonmel Countess won the Convivial Plate, and Haverty and Mr O'Hagan had her backed at forty to one. Mr Coyne had gone for Sally's Pippin. In the outhouse that is still a workshop the mahogany dressing-table, once taken from Colonel Rolleston's bedroom to have a leg repaired, is lost beneath the paint tins and bottles that clutter it. 'This stuff's worth a fortune, you know,' Haverty said on one of the occasions he and Tom had to go on to the roof to repair the lead. You could repair a pinprick perforation by touching it with Seccotine or Durafix, but when the perforations were larger, or there were cracks, there wasn't much you could do except to catch the drips. 'We'd feel happier if you were in the house with us,' Villana said when only she and Sarah Pollexfen were left. Tom sleeps in the room that was his father's, and sits with Patty in the kitchen in the evenings. Six months ago the slates began to fall away from the roof of the gate-lodge.

'I have things to do,' Tom says in the kitchen, and is

followed by his dog to the fields. The ground is hard, like iron beneath his feet. When he feels for the moist clay of the well he finds it turned to ice. On the ledge of rock that was once level with his eye, but which he looks down on now, the cache of crucifixes and coins has been added to over the years, but those he remembers from his childhood are still there. Every year still, in high summer, the women come. Ever since the death occurred he has been intending to make this visit.

Near by, his sheep huddle under a broken wall; he counts them as he passes. Five there are; fifteen he has counted on the side of the hill; others graze the grass beneath the monkey puzzle and the strawberry trees. His cattle winter in the cobbled yard.

He walks the fields, examining his fences. In the crook of his arm, protected by a piece of sacking, he carries a coil of barbed wire. A gate, rotten twelve months ago, collapses when he attempts to move it on its hinges; there are places where the posts must be renewed. The grass may perhaps be better this year than it was last if the ragwort does not increase. Little yellow boy, Sister Teresa Dolores called it, touching with the tip of her cane the chart on the blackboard. *Buachallán buí.*

He pulls a length of wire taut, gripping it with his pliers, then hammers in another staple. The frost which had earlier been white on the grass has gone; his footsteps, to and from the fence, have marked a path. He has always known that he would have the house when Sarah Pollexfen died.

In the kitchen Patty cuts slices of yesterday's bacon. On the electric stove that has replaced the range a saucepan of potatoes boils. The dresser and the long oak table are as they'd been for as long as she can remember, the same icy draught blowing in from the scullery passage. Since the death, Patty has been quiet, not saying much to Tom. Her knuckles on the panels of Sarah Pollexfen's door had resounded without response, the cup of tea she carried steaming in the cold air. She had not opened the door when there was no reply to her raised voice, but had gone for Tom instead.

She lays two places at the kitchen table and turns the radio on. Men's voices argue about farm prices; she does not listen, and in a moment turns it off again. What will Tom do now? It is no secret that Esmeralda Coyne would marry him. Many times after Mass on Sundays, when people stand about and talk, Patty has heard it said that Esmeralda Coyne would marry him and try to turn Carriglas into some kind of hotel.

'I have to go over this afternoon,' Tom says when they have eaten the food that has been prepared.

Patty does not care for being left alone in the house with the body still laid out, but she does not say so. She will remain in the kitchen. She will not leave it until he returns.

'Will you get the bread, and pork chops in Broderick's? Get four good chops with the kidney in them.'

He says he will. She writes down other items on a scrap torn off the edge of a newspaper. He is going over to bet, she guesses: nothing that happens can prevent him from laying down his bets. Still freckled and still incredulous about the eyes, though a grey-haired woman now, Patty has never in her life gambled on a horse or a greyhound: all that is a man's thing.

He drives to the town, across the bridge, his black dog sprawled on the seat beside him. Empty trees stand bleakly, against the sharp blue of a sky that is clear of clouds. Smoke from the few houses he passes rises straight; frost lingers beneath the hedges.

As he approaches the town he raises a hand often in salutation; he is as well known as anyone for miles around. He draws the car up at Spillane's public house. 'A bottle of stout,' he orders at the bar. He greets the men who are there, and nods when the barman says: 'I hear she died.'

'She did.'

A man looks up from the *Irish Press*. He'd heard that too, he says, and decently lets time elapse before he adds: 'Lashaway to win, Tom?'

Wiping froth from his lips, Tom nods again. He intends to place a bet on Lashaway: he has a feeling in his bones about that horse. The man with the newspaper laughs. 'I heard that one before, Tom.'

'She'll win all right.'

Ever since he read in the diaries about the events that followed his father's death Tom has been trying to comprehend them. Dowley found the excuse for his vengeance in the troubles there were, and that was natural enough. But the extraordinariness of what happened next bewilders Tom. There'd always been talk of the Rollestons slaughtering their way to the island, but there'd been talk as well of how they'd been decent at the time of the Famine, and they'd been decent to his mother and they'd been decent to him. Funny the way a thing like the other would afflict them, the way they couldn't come to terms with it.

'You won't get much in the way of odds,' the man with the newspaper warns, and Tom replies that he knows he won't. Other horses are discussed. Little Jack Horner and Funnyface III. Sky-Writer, Fred Wootton up. 'Would the funeral be in the morning?' the barman enquires, drying a glass.

'Eleven o'clock.'

'Ah, well.'

Tom finishes his drink, and does not speak again except to say he'll be back later on. In Byrne's he gets odds of eleven to eight. He takes the ticket and leaves the turf accountant's, even though he could watch the race if he stayed there. He always prefers not to do that; it's become a habit with him to place his bet and then to go away, to walk about and do what shopping is necessary while the race is run.

'A good age,' Esmeralda Coyne remarks, stopping him to say it. 'Was it peaceful with her?'

'I think maybe she went in her sleep.'

'It's nice like that.'

He says it is. He knows that Esmeralda Coyne is inquisitive about what is going to happen now. More than ten years have passed since she remarked, meeting him as casually as this, that people couldn't help how they came into the world, how could they? Nobody these days gave tuppence about a thing like that, she'd said.

'It's a grand old house they've left behind, Tom.'

'It's shook enough in places.'

'It wouldn't take much to put it right.'

She does not disguise her interest. Whenever people in the shops or the public houses look at him in a certain way he knows Esmeralda Coyne has come into their minds. The oldest of her sisters married Slattery, who'd taught Tom how to climb up and look through the billiard-hall windows. They have the garage and the petrol pump now, and Esmeralda lives in the house with them.

'A hotel's the coming thing in Ireland, Tom. The Yanks are here in droves.'

'I've heard it, all right.'

'We'll pull the blinds down for her funeral.'

On the promenade two nuns dressed differently from Sister Teresa Dolores and Sister Sullivan walk briskly. It's hard to become used to the dress they wear now, not to think of them as lay workers of some kind. They glance in his direction, but do not greet him. It's well known that he puts in time on the promenade while a race is being run, that afterwards he'll return to Spillane's for an hour or so, win or lose. He wonders if the nuns remark that he is feckless, wasting time when he should be working. Being unmarried himself, he has something in common with them, but they cannot be expected to see that, any more than Sister Teresa Dolores or Sister Sullivan might once have felt they occupied a common ground with Briscoe or Mr McGrath and Mr Tobin of the Rose of Tralee boarding-house. Briscoe married in the end, and so did Mr Tobin, but Mr McGrath did not, nor did Mr O'Hagan, and the ferryman was always too old. Tom has never wanted to marry himself, Esmeralda Coyne or anyone else. 'There's some like that by nature,' the ferryman used to say, the subject of bachelors always a favourite with him. He had not meant priests, of course. He had excluded the ruling of a priest's vocation.

Shops have crept into the promenade; a supermarket sprawls. The old billiard-hall has been demolished. The wasteland that was to have been the Father Quirke Park is still a wasteland.

He turns and walks back again, past the brass plates and the window where the white cat stared out disdainfully. Not far from here he had his last conversation with Holy Mullihan before Holy Mullihan left the town. Fifty yards further on, Traynor's Picture Palace is a furniture store.

In Byrne's he collects his winnings and then buys the items on Patty's list in Meath's, asking for a plastic bag to carry them in. The woman at the till mentions the death, respectfully commiserating. 'Lonely for you now,' she speculates as she punches out the prices on the cash register, and he replies that perhaps it will be. Her eyes pass over his clothes when she turns to tell him what the total is, and he can feel her thinking that Esmeralda Coyne should be looking after them. He has put a jacket on, as he always does when he drives over: with his trousers, it makes a suit, brown, striped, creased and shiny in places. The green jersey he wears is tattered at the elbows but cannot be seen beneath the jacket. 'Is Patty still across?' the woman casually asks.

'She is.'

'I didn't see her this long time.'

The woman is wondering if it is right and proper for

Patty and himself to remain under the one roof, now that Sarah Pollexfen has died. She is wondering if Esmeralda Coyne knows enough about the business to take charge of an hotel. She is wondering if Esmeralda Coyne will get him.

Tom knows all that. He can sense the woman's thoughts because he has known that woman all his life. He packs the items he has bought into a carrier bag and says goodbye to her. She calls after him to ask the day of the funeral. 'Tomorrow,' he says.

There's hardly enough land left to scrape a living from. Between them the brothers sold too much after Lionel's accident with the harvester, and then again when Haverty was too old to work. They had needed the money to keep the household going, and none of it had mattered since there wasn't going to be another generation. One of these days he will try to buy an acre or two back.

In Broderick's he watches the pork chops being cut, a section of kidney left on each. The butcher, son of the Broderick who sent over meat of poor quality to Carriglas, being upset because his wife was pregnant, remarks upon the death, and sympathises. 'Tomorrow,' Tom repeats. The doors of the shop will be closed, he is assured.

'No trouble in the world.' In Spillane's the barman's tone is complimentary. 'An easy length.'

'The going suited her, of course.'

His stout is poured. The man who'd been reading the *Irish Press* has gone. What'll become of the old place? the barman conversationally enquires, and Tom remembers what Haverty said about the lead on the roof being worth a fortune, and Villana saying once: 'Sell Carriglas for the lead, Tom.' He doesn't know, he replies.

He drinks for a while longer; other matters are talked about. Then he picks up the plastic bag of groceries and makes his way back to where he has parked the car. Dusk is gathering; the air is colder than it has been all day; the sky has reddened in the west. In the car he strokes the dog's head before he starts the engine. Its tail wags, thumping against the door of the car. 'Aren't you the patient fellow?' he says, the praise the dog likes best.

Dusk gathers as he drives through the countryside. On the bridge the bronze plate that honours a hero has been dulled by time. Lichen has crept on to the concrete it's set in. He passes by, unaffected by its presence.

'Is it still cold?' Patty enquires, unpacking the groceries.

'It is.'

'Did you see anyone?'

He mentions the barman in Spillane's and the man reading the *Irish Press*, and the woman who'd engaged him in conversation at the till in Meath's. He makes no reference to Esmeralda Coyne because there is no need to. 'Broderick's will close their doors,' he says. In the closer of the two sculleries he prepares a plate of food for his dog and then returns to await his own food at the table.

She opens a tin of peaches he has bought and spoons the fruit on to two plates. The chops are fried, slices of fresh bread cut. Tea is made.

Patty guesses that Esmeralda Coyne was on the watch out for him. She'd have known he'd be over because she'd have looked in the papers to see what races were running. She'd have said something because the death would have prompted it.

'The horse I had came in,' he says.

'Did you win much, Tom?'

'Not much. Only it came in when I knew it would. I was pleased about that.'

He, too, is pondering the future. You could have a hotel and strangers would walk through the rooms that had been the Rollestons'. You would make a profit. The visitors would come with their luggage, as the visitors had at the time of the wedding, only all of it would be easier because of the bridge being there. They would drink whiskey in the hall and sit down to their dinner. You'd grow vegetables for them in the garden. One day, ages ago, Esmeralda Coyne laid it all out for him. The island would be different then, a new place altogether, with all that coming and going. And Esmeralda is young enough to have a child or two.

'Ah, great,' he says as his chops are placed before him. The black dog is stretched out by the door. An alarm clock ticks on the dresser.

'What was the name of the horse, Tom?'

'Lashaway. A young filly.'

'It's good she won.'

As she eats, an irony occurs to Patty: it seems odd that a hearse should take the body back to the mainland when the whole island was a burial place once. It was Sarah Pollexfen herself who'd told her that, who'd explained in the kitchen one afternoon about the standing stones. She'd spoken of the graveyard beneath them, and the boats that carried the dead to this chosen place, the processing of the funerals.

'I never saw the standing stones,' she says. 'I never was up there.'

'They'll be there a while yet.'

'I'll go up one of these days.'

Somehow it will be easier now. Sarah Pollexfen was the gentlest of creatures, but she was there to give an order and to restrain. It seems a pity to destroy her diaries, Patty reflects as she clears away the dishes, even though she said they might be destroyed when they were read. Fancy a maid from this kitchen sending in demands for money!

'It's dry in the cupboard by the range,' she suggests. 'As good a place as any.'

Tom nods in agreement. For an hour he reads the newspaper, spread out on the table where the plates and cups have been. There was an emptiness, too, when the others went, one by one. He sensed it again this morning when he passed through the yard, and when he took the short cut through the garden and walked on the road to the pier. It will last a month or two, and then it won't be noticeable any more.

'Goodnight so, Tom,' Patty bids him, taking the alarm clock from the dresser.

They will live here, changing nothing: they both know that now, though neither says it. He will not sell the lead from the roof, any more than he'll ask Burke's to come over and arrange an auction. In time people will become used to the two of them having a home in the same house. In time Esmeralda Coyne's interest will wither. 'You are happy, Tom?' Villana said, the time she asked him to leave the gate-lodge for the house. He wanted nothing more than what he had, he confessed. 'Oh, that is happiness,' Villana said.

'Goodnight, Patty.'

He remains a moment longer, then climbs the back stairs, turning lights on as he goes. In the bedroom that is fusty with the odour of death he folds back the edge of the sheet and gazes into the pallid face. Already it is not Sarah Pollexfen's, but in the presence of the dwindling likeness he is grateful that she made the contribution of a poor relation to a family's epitaph. *Carriglas will be a place to stroll to on a summer's afternoon*, the tidy script asserts, *as we have strolled to the fallen abbey and the burial mound. Absence has gathered in the rooms, and silence in the garden. They have returned Carriglas to its clay.* He covers again the still remains and moves to extinguish the light. As he descends through the house those last words echo, lightening his bewilderment: their punishment of themselves seems terrible, yet a marvel also.

FOR THE BEST IN PAPERBACKS, LOOK FOR THE

A CHOICE OF PENGUIN FICTION

The Captain and the Enemy   Graham Greene

The Captain always maintained that he won Jim from his father at a game of backgammon … 'It is good to find the best living writer … still in such first-rate form' – Francis King in the *Spectator*

The Book and the Brotherhood   Iris Murdoch

'Why should we go on supporting a book which we detest?' Rose Curtland asks. 'The brotherhood of Western intellectuals versus the book of history,' Jenkin Riderhood suggests. 'A thoroughly gripping, stimulating and challenging fiction' – *The Times*

The Image and Other Stories   Isaac Bashevis Singer

'These touching, humorous, beautifully executed stories are the work of a true artist' – *Daily Telegraph*. 'Singer's robust new collection of tales shows a wise teacher at his best' – *Mail on Sunday*

The Enigma of Arrival   V. S. Naipaul

'For sheer abundance of talent, there can hardly be a writer alive who surpasses V. S. Naipaul. Whatever we want in a novelist is to be found in his books' – Irving Howe in *The New York Times Book Review*

Earthly Powers   Anthony Burgess

Anthony Burgess's masterpiece: an enthralling, epic narrative spanning six decades and spotlighting some of the most vivid events and characters of our time. 'Enormous imagination and vitality … a huge book in every way' – Bernard Levin in the *Sunday Times*

A CHOICE OF PENGUIN FICTION

A Theft   Saul Bellow

Subtle and tense, the tale of the passionate Clara Velde and her stolen ring. 'The warmth, the kindness, the tenderness of *A Theft* overpower criticism' – *Sunday Telegraph*

Incline Our Hearts   A. N. Wilson

'An account of an eccentric childhood so moving, so private and personal, and so intensely funny that it bears inescapable comparison with that greatest of childhood novels, *David Copperfield*' – *Daily Telegraph*

Three Continents   Ruth Prawer Jhabvala

Last-of-line scions of a prominent American family, spoilt, blindly idealistic and extremely rich, Harriet and her twin brother Michael seem set to prove perfect fodder for the charismatic Rawul of Dhoka and his sinister Sixth World Movement. 'A writer of world class' – *Sunday Times*

The New Confessions   William Boyd

The outrageous, hilarious autobiography of John James Todd, a Scotsman born in 1899 and one of the great self-appointed (and failed) geniuses of the twentieth century. 'Brilliant … a Citizen Kane of a novel' – *Daily Telegraph*

Maia   Richard Adams

The heroic romance of love and war in an ancient empire from one of our greatest storytellers. 'Enormous and powerful' – *Sunday Times*

The News From Ireland

Subtle, observant, probing, these short stories confirm William Trevor as a master of the genre. 'Trevor packs into each separate five or six thousand words more richness, more laughter, more ache, more multifarious human-ness than many good writers manage to get into a whole novel' – *Punch*

The Children of Dynmouth

A small, pretty seaside town is harshly exposed by a young boy's curiosity. His prurient interest, oddly motivated, leaves few people unaffected – and the consequences cannot be ignored.

The Boarding House

By selecting carefully, William Wagner Bird filled his boarding house with people that society would never miss – even if it noticed they were around. But then he made a fatal mistake. He died.

Fools of Fortune

Spanning sixty years, William Trevor's tender and beautiful love story has at its centre a dark and violent act which spills over into the mutilated lives of generations to come. 'To my mind William Trevor's best novel and a very fine one' – Graham Greene

Other People's Worlds

William Trevor's pellucid prose and elegant craftsmanship coolly lead the reader into the pathological world of Francis Tyte – a world where his secret and shabby fantasies feed destructively on his victims. 'One may turn to him always for artistry, wisdom and wit' – *Sunday Telegraph*

Also published

Elizabeth Alone
The Love Department
Mrs Eckdorf in O'Neill's Hotel
The Old Boys
The Stories of William Trevor